LOST IN VEGAS

EDWARD ANCHEL

iUNIVERSE, INC.
NEW YORK   BLOOMINGTON

Lost in Vegas

iUniverse books may be ordered through booksellers or by contacting:

iUniverse
1663 Liberty Drive
Bloomington, IN 47403
www.iuniverse.com
1-800-Authors (1-800-288-4677)

ISBN: 978-1-4502-3366-8 (sc)
ISBN: 978-1-4502-3368-2 (dj)
ISBN: 978-1-4502-3367-5 (ebk)

Printed in the United States of America

iUniverse rev. date: 6/14/2010

ACKNOWLEDGEMENTS

To Dad, the leader of my band, so that my children, theirs and theirs.......
will know how much I loved you and them.

To Ellen, Dawn, Larry and Marc who provided the love, inspiration,
and input allowing me to undertake this project. Unfortunately, you
unavoidably will have to endure its contents.

To Marjorie Fennessy who painted the stunning portrait of my
father.

To Doc, Scott Erickson, who shared countless hours with me over
this project, but not in Las Vegas.

To Carol Goodman who gently made it clear that I should have paid
more attention to Mrs. Fleckenstein's grammar lessons.

To Tracy Sims, my instructor for, "How to Write a Book in Six
Weeks", it took a little longer, but thanks for your motivation, I think
I graduated.

Thank you.

PREFACE

Oh shit, the calendar says it is only Wednesday. That can't be. Wasn't it Wednesday yesterday? This is like watching molasses flow in the winter. Is Friday ever going to get here?

Anticipating my Friday; At 11:00 AM I would deliver my bride, Elaine, to her friend Susan's house so that they could begin their Caribbean Cruise; from there I would be off to Palm Beach International Airport to commence my adventure in Las Vegas. Too bad Doc took ill and would not accompany me. Considering that he is a doctor, he tended to be sick for these outings way too often. Should I have stayed home? Nah, I do so love my pilgrimages to Nevada's version of Mecca and, notwithstanding being solo, I could not pass up on my marital freedom for the long week-end.

I am not sure that I was particularly productive those waning days, but I did manage to clear my desk of superfluous papers, sign off on some filings for a pending engagement, and provide final billing instructions for the trial that I completed last week. Atlas, Immerson and Sheering, Attorneys at Law would have to do without its senior partner until next Tuesday. I hung up my "Gone Fishin" sign and grabbed the next elevator to freedom.

'Twas finally Friday and we were in the car; Elaine babbling about jewelry shopping, Pina Coladas and long days being kissed by the sun on various island beaches. My mind's reverie sees only stacks of chips accumulated during wondrous gaming sessions. I feared that her expectations would more closely align with reality.

Predictably, the departures board at PBI indicated that Delta Flight 711 was delayed an estimated hour, which ultimately became three. Number two on the minus chart of reasons to stay home. Undaunted, I passed the hours at Sam Snead's Lounge tasting the fine selections of vodkas on their shelf. With only thirty minutes 'til departure time, I ventured over to the gate only to find that I would have been the next first class upgrade if another seat was available, but the dark cloud of fortune once again blocked the sun and I would be forced to sit in the back of the plane, not my favorite place to be. Reason number three!

Finally in Vegas, my chariot, a Checker Cab is summoned to bring me to the tables to fulfill my fantasies. I disclosed my destination, the Paris Hotel and Casino to the driver and I was off. Rather than waiting for the hotel's Parisian café, the cabbie suggested that I start my escape immediately and offered me a drink. A drink in a cab? This would never happen in Florida, but I was not in Kansas anymore; I accepted the cup. With hindsight, having the benefit of later reviewing the events as they unfolded, I cannot justify that decision. However, at the time I viewed such offering as a great way to start my weekend. I was wrong!

The liquid I consumed in his cab was clear and tasted like vodka, but even though it only filled half the plastic cup, it was obviously the strongest I ever consumed. It had the punch of a double or triple, and seemed so much stronger. The radio was not playing, but I kept hearing repeating stanzas of the Beatles' "Lucy in the Sky with Diamonds."

Didn't he just pass the exit for my hotel? Wasn't that the Stratosphere Hotel we just passed? We were almost downtown; where the hell was he taking me?

Why didn't I heed the omens and stay home?

CHAPTER ONE

TUESDAY MORNING

Not bad for a Brooklyn Boy! Gazing out of my seventeenth floor office window I view a wondrous panoramic vista spanning the opulent Intercoastal Waterway in Palm Beach; complete with swaying palm trees, an impressive array of mansions, and a seemingly endless parade of water vessels. I have often lauded myself about what I have accomplished before my fifty-fifth birthday. Such perch and the hypnotizing effect of water serve as catalysts for my many daily doses of escapism. However, the endless demands of managing a law firm tip the scales in the other direction, bringing me back to reality.

As I reflect on those mind numbing hours in Professors Gallagher and Person's classes providing lullabies through Securities and Patent Law, I often wonder why those two specialties rose to the top and became the nucleus of my career. Wouldn't it have been easier to take accounting and become a Certified Public Accountant?

Alas, this is South Florida perhaps the largest per-capita scam center of America, and when the scammers take a nap, our focus shifts to our sub-specialty. There has always been an ample diet of intellectual property matters available to fill the slack and keep our partners and ten associates grinding away.

On my desk I noticed yesterday, September 6, 2004's edition of The South Florida Law Journal. They ran a two column story on the cover

1

page describing the case we concluded last week successfully defending a local discount brokerage firm and four of its salesmen against charges of account churning. I detest those scoundrel attorneys, Ambulance Chasers, who plaster billboards and local radio and television with ads seeking clients. There has to be a better way to build a practice. They could do it the old fashioned way, *They Could Earn It*. Instead, they prey on the greed of humanity and often find themselves shooting fish in a barrel. It is human nature to desire replacement of lost funds. However, it is often the plaintiff who should bear at least some of the responsibility for such losses, rather than taking the easy road and sue the ones with deep pockets.

Most of these cases are settled out of court yielding revenues for the shysters and their client minions. We at AI&S long ago established a policy of litigating these matters rather than settling most cases in this genre. Such protocol does occasionally cost our clients more in legal fees, but our track record has been very successful and many of the outcomes have resulted in minimal or no cash awards to the plaintiffs.

We had been featured in various articles, some even national in scope (at least fifteen times during the past last year) and are rapidly becoming a force to be reckoned with in the legal community. Today's article was so flattering to our firm's technical knowledge and litigating acumen that I jotted a suggestion on a Post-it indicating that we should order 300 reprints and send them out with our monthly invoices. The expense incurred in delivering this message would be minimal; the goodwill to be generated would be priceless!

On a personal level, I found the last three paragraphs of the clip very enticing; the columnist presented something of keen interest to me. Although, to date, I had only heard about it in hints and rumors, he wrote that the Tallahassee GOP machine had stepped up their lobbying to Governor. They always want an enhanced Floridian presence in D.C. and were coaxing Jeb to speak with his brother concerning placing my name in consideration to fill the recently vacated seat on the Securities and Exchange Commission. The last sentence of the piece suggested that such movement was gaining traction.

Why would they pick me, a closet Democrat? Registered as an Independent voter, I had always attempted to stay out of the political fray. Both through the firm and personally, I had made obligatory contributions to both major parties. After all, it pays to have friends on both sides of the aisle. My on-the-surface ambivalence may have paid off; Bush, the President, is barred from naming another Republican to the Commission, and his brother, Bush, the Governor, apparently wanted, or was being cajoled into suggesting me for the vacancy.

Kicking off my shoes, I lifted my legs up on the desk and re-read the piece prior to tossing it my out-basket with the Post-it firmly affixed. Peering out my window I was once again mesmerized by my good fortune and the calming waterway at the base of our building. Perhaps I spend too much of my day reflecting this way. Humbug! I do juggle my virtual and real worlds into a workable, albeit questionable state of equilibrium.

Given the recent stimuli, I could have drifted back to Gainesville boasting to my mentors, I could have chosen the White house accepting W's generous offer, or countless other scenarios. However, I returned to my modest roots and found myself back in Flatbush playing stickball in the gated school-yard at P.S. (Public School, for those of you who did not grow up in the environs of New York City) 53. I noticed that Miss Fox, not just my fifth grade teacher, but more appropriately, Aphrodite incarnate, was watching my every move from the fifth floor library window; I had to do good. No doubt this would evolve into yet another sophomoric journey into the fantasies of a hormonally developing eleven year old boy.

What a shot! That pink Spaulding was hurtling over the fence with so much height and velocity that I was at second base by the time I heard the cheers for my prowess. Another game saving homer by the David, the champ rescuing the East 12th Street bombers from the crap we would have faced had we lost to the 13th Street Assholes, or whatever their name was. Before I reached home plate, I looked skyward to confirm that she was still there. She was, and I immediately began wondering how Miss Fox would reward my athleticism in class tomorrow.

Having the name Atlas, throughout my education, I usually found myself in the first seat of the first row. In Miss Fox's class this put me a mere fifteen feet and forty-five degrees from the most beautiful woman in the world. There I was awaiting her grand entrance to the room.

Would she wear a particularly revealing blouse or offer me one of her elongated swivels providing the best of up-skirt shots? A safer choice would have been her confirmation to the class that she knew that I would one day be batting in clean-up position for the Brooklyn Dodgers. The earlier choices would always be my preference; at that age I knew that my destiny included a white and blue uniform having Ebbets Field as a second home and Duke Snider as a best bud.

My pre-pubescent and post post-pubescent fantasies, a good way to encompass all, generally favor sensuality over practicality.

The door opened and the goddess glided into view. She was not only wearing my favorite skirt, but also the sexiest of blouses. I knew that I would have a wonderful day. My mind was immediately envisioning dropped pieces of chalk and her requisite bending down to retrieve same. Heart be still! Oh, she was getting ready to take attendance. She was rolling away from her desk. Her chair was pivoting toward me and all I could think about is what color panties she was wearing and… and….

Like the screeching of an alarm clock at 6:00 AM, "David, PICK UP, Elaine is on line 3", bellowed Rachel, my secretary of eight years was indicating that Elaine, my wife of almost thirty years, was on hold. Up went the receiver and down went my erection.

Foregoing the many treats Miss Fox would undoubtedly have doled out that day, albeit not voluntarily, I responded, "Hi babe, what's cooking?" Such response was almost always my opening line. It must be true; in reality I am a predictable and not a very creative guy. In fact my friend Rick says that I have a near boring personality. I always found relative comfort in that near boring was better than being there!

Elaine was unbridled and her enthusiastically charged message was, "Susan just called and told me Bob cannot get away for their cruise this week-end. He has to go see his mom in New York and help her resolve a problem involving the co-op she co-signed with his brother Louis. Since they cannot get their money back from Carnival, she asked if I wanted go in his place. What do you think?"

"Where's the cruise going, how long would you be gone?" I responded feigning interest. Who cared about Louis or Susan's mom losing money? My thoughts immediately went to an opening window for a trip to Las Vegas and wondering if Maggie would allow Doc to join me for a western sojourn.

"Only for the week-end, out Friday back on Monday. I know that you and I have been all over the Caribbean, but this would be with Susan and you know how long we have been talking about going away together. Come on, please, I'll make it up to you." Elaine clearly wanted this and certainly would not contest my concurrent journey westward, and beside, she was going to make it up to me.

Instinctively, my response was "Sure thing babe, tell her O.K. You'll have a ball". Before saying good bye, I was already keying in Doc's number on my cell phone. "I'll be home between 6:00 – 6:30. Start packing, See ya. Gotta go." Did I ask her what was on the menu for dinner? Who cared?

I am truly a multi-tasking master. With one hand on the Intercom, "Rachel call Delta and find out my flight choices this Friday afternoon; PBI – LAS returning on Tuesday morning's red-eye". Speaking into my cell, "Hi Doc, hold on;" into the intercom, "Rachel let me know ASAP."

Doc is my closest friend, Dr. Lamont Silver, one of Fort Lauderdale's leading vascular surgeons. We met during our freshman year at University of Florida and have been like brothers ever since even though I finished my undergraduate days in Miami. It was during those early pre-med years that I dubbed him with the nickname "Doc"; it rolls off the tongue easier than Lamont.

How was it that a Brooklyn boy, actually a Long Island boy, by the time college rolled around, wound up at Florida? Not proud to admit it but, I moved in with my Aunt Beatrice in Miami, and changed my residency in order to afford me the opportunity to afford an education as a Gator.

Silver remained in Gainesville to earn his Bachelors Degree in Pre-Med while I completed my four-year stint as a Hurricane at the University of Miami. Although she is no longer with us, my aunt Bea exerted major influence and obtained a scholarship causing my southbound journey and final two years in Coral Gables. A month after graduation and prior to finalizing law school plans, I received my Greetings Notice from the United States Army offering me a short detour from education.

Back in the States two years later, with the wisdom and maturity that one receives during a two year sentence to Army discipline and

Vietnam's rigors, I returned to my Gator roots and completed Law School in Alachua County, compliments of the Veterans Administration. Doc being much more worldly, financially secure, and free from the perils of the draft went north to Emory in Atlanta for Medical training. Many years and experiences thereafter we resumed our friendship as we both commenced our respective careers in Fort Lauderdale.

While he was in Atlanta, he met and married Maggie, a third grade teacher in the Fulton County, Atlanta School System. Getting tired of the long distance romance, I married my high school sweetheart, Elaine, also a teacher, during my final year of Law School. Kindergarten was her choice; she is great with kids. One would think that given the similarity, the girls would have been just as close as Doc and me. However, oil and water do not mix and they never got along; no matter, each respects our friendship and allows it to flourish.

"Doc, the Vegas window has opened for this week-end. Elaine is going away with Susan. What are the chances that Maggie will cut you loose?" Although short, I was sure that he got the message. We both wanted this trip; a western-bonding and often plotted the possibilities of how it would happen.

His response, "It is already Tuesday, not much notice. Exactly what days do I have to beg for?"

I offered a short synopsis of Elaine's itinerary and told him that I intended to stretch it a little by returning on Monday's Red-eye. With the five-plus hour in-flight nap available on an over-night schedule, we would arrive home by 7:00 AM Tuesday both ready to cut hearts, of course in our differing venues, as we do best.

"Bring home flowers, tell her to invite her mother to spend the week-end at your place or come up with a plan of your own. Do whatever it takes," I suggested. We had each been to Vegas multiple times, even at the same times with our brides. On those occasions, Maggie and Elaine always avoided a hotel that they knew the other to be at; leaving Doc and me to arrange our mutual rendezvous.

Doc and I have often gone for overnights to Atlantic City or the Bahamas, but this would be our first venture to Vegas together sans spouses. We both married Jewish girls and accordingly were and are destined to go through gyrations whenever we want something not originally suggested by the wife. Fortunately, I had the pass and it was

Doc who had to jump through hoops in order to earn permission. His predicament was another entry in the imaginary saga that we were yet to publish, *Ode to the Jewish Husband.*

He assured me that he would do his best and get back to me by tomorrow. I assessed the situation and calculated a fifty percent probability of success. However, the deck was stacked. If I had known that Maggie had just seen her mother last week-end, I would have dropped the line to thirty percent.

I looked at my watch and recognized that I could not spend much more time on my Vegas arrangements. It was almost 11:30 and I had less than thirty minutes to complete the agenda for our partners' meeting. We had a similar caucus every month over luncheon on the first Tuesday of each month. Thankfully, I remembered yesterday to have Rachel order sandwiches and assorted goodies for the two hour session, affording us an opportunity to review events of the past and coming month while devouring the best of local cuisine.

I do not usually leave important matters such as strategic firm planning for the last minute. However, this month I almost had an excuse. What's more important: Promoting Judith Kaplan, our highest billing associate, to partner or planning my Vegas escapade and spending a few moments with Miss Fox? Judith would have to wait at least another month to learn if she will become the first female to join our currently male only fraternal partnership.

Although some might challenge my executive abilities in managing the firm's affairs, we have prospered, grown, and have established a great reputation; it generally works quite well.

I gathered last month's billing runs, the accounts receivable listings, current work-in-progress reports, scanned my calendar for meetings, hearings, depositions already scheduled during the coming weeks and got ready to run off to the conference room. Fortunately, I remembered to put my shoes back on and straighten my tie, ensuring a look of professionalism prior to arriving at the meeting.

CHAPTER TWO

Tuesday afternoon

I would have preferred being the first to arrive, but Brent, Brent Immerson, beat me to the punch. He was sitting in one of our decorator's favorite purchases, fourteen plush attorney-brown leather chairs; his perched next to the head of the table, a spot reserved for me. He was reading the Palm Beach Post's sports pages, I would have been happier if it were the Law Journal.

Aside from being the first to arrive, Brent was my first and therefore my longest standing partner. For years we practiced as Atlas & Immerson. He would have preferred being the first named partner arguing that Immerson & Atlas had a better ring to it. He may have been right, but I had the higher billings, my name was alphabetically first and I always wanted to be a first named partner; my ego was just as enlarged as was his. All logic aside, the final vote was cast as I called heads and George Washington's pretty face landed on the desk facing skyward.

Brent's birth day and year are within days of mine. More importantly, his strongest attributes and mine complemented each others. In the early days, we were quite a tag team He was more socially assertive and I was the more cerebral one. When meeting a potential new client, we worked together perfectly, hand-in-hand. His task was to charmingly break the ice and my technical dexterity generally closed the deal. This led me think that our partnership was destined for success; he achieved the

8

brotherly status in my life theretofore only enjoyed by Doc. Although I have a biological Brother, Donald, my relationships with Doc and Brent were far more intimate.

The barrier with Immerson, although not a deal-breaker, came about a year after we formalized our association. He confided that he was currently and had been, for several years, in an extramarital relationship. Making the matter worse, she was one of our clients. I generously refer to her as a client even though her annual billings rarely exceeded five thousand dollars. This disclosure made our two couple social outings with Elaine and Jennifer, his wife, difficult. Actually, the girls got along just fine. Each was equally ignorant of the outside relationship. Ignorance is bliss! I, on the other hand, was not blissful. I viewed his indiscretion as a major personality flaw and constantly wondered how it would affect us professionally.

Although somewhat able to compartmentalize his behavior, I did wish that he would change his ways and keep *IT* in his pants. I was explaining that to him last week-end at a dinner party hosted by a mutual friend. I was sharing how difficult it was for me to see Jennifer while hiding his secret. He indicated that I should not concern myself about his affairs, or should I have said business, when I noticed Jennifer approaching and quickly changed the subject. By the time she joined us, we were talking about his favorite subject, his golf swing.

The paradigm in the Atlas household has always been no cheating, no beating, no excuses; Elaine's Mandate! It was the unquestionable foundation supporting our relationship. My love for her is paramount. My relationship with my children would surely suffer; under any circumstance, there is little doubt that they would side with her if this promise were breached. The combination of the wrath of God and the wrath of Elaine; I do not know which is worse, would make my life a horrific hell. Accordingly, these factors formed and continue to form the non-breachable trifecta of armor assuring my fidelity.

I had a hard time understanding Brent's reasoning for distancing himself from me. I knew my reasons. However, without tooting my horn, he was clearly the winner by pairing up with me. He surely would not be where he was, were it not for the opportunities originated and closed by his partner. Notwithstanding, we were and are partners and I preferred the erstwhile days to the present, as it related to our relationship.

Ed Sheerson, chronologically the third partner of our firm entered the room within a minute of the stipulated commencement time. Although always punctual and reliable, Ed still felt compelled to explain his tardiness. He is probably the most compulsive and honest member of our firm. Notwithstanding these fine traits, I would guess that he charged the client he was talking with on the phone an extra half hour for causing him the embarrassment of being late. What silliness! We were not even ready to start, Tepperman and Shields, our two unnamed partners were yet to show up.

Ed was a member of my congregation. We lived two streets apart, our children were the same ages and went through the Coral Springs School System together from middle school through high school and, over the years, we had frequently shared many outings both socially and professionally. Our families lived in Broward County during those fledgling years of practice development, but both had our practices based in Boca Raton. Our ultimate association appeared destined.

Shortly after joining forces, Ed usurped Brent's position becoming my closest partner in both the personal and business matters. He also was aware of Brent's dalliance, had a similar attitude of disapproval, and was also able to look the other way. It was rarely spoken about aloud, but I would guess that most of the staff directly or indirectly had some knowledge of Brent's inappropriate relationship. It was amazing that he was able to keep it from Jennifer all those years.

Not long after merger, it became apparent that we had outgrown our office in suburban Boca Raton. We skipped over a town or two and settled into our current Flagler Drive site; in one of Palm Beach's most trendy new buildings, a stone's throw from the County Court House where we most often found ourselves litigating. Although further north, the Interstate and Turnpike offered a logistically acceptable location close enough to the federal and state jurisdictions in the counties to our south. Not surprisingly, as our kids left for college and beyond, the empty nest syndrome set in, and we both moved our personal residences to Boca Raton.

Jesse Tepperman was an associate in Ed's previous firm, a tightly run three man legal boutique specializing in Securities matters. He came along when Sheerson amalgamated with us. Jesse is younger than the three of us, controls a smaller book of billings, but is a knowledgeable technician with a quick and logical mind which added great depth to our team. Initially he joined us as a Senior Associate and was asked to join the partnership two years ago.

Douglas Shields represents our most recent partner. He practiced alone with a secretary specializing in the field of Intellectual Property. Over the past years we have been attracting new clients in this area. As we developed this niche, we required additional talent, and felt that his personality and skill set meshed nicely with ours. Accordingly, last April we coaxed him into moving from Boca Raton to West Palm Beach to merge with our firm.

It was and continues to be a major element of my personality that I need to be in control; unless, of course control is beyond my reach. Such was not the case at AI&S or so I thought.

I often viewed dealing with the personalities of my four partners as being in a cage; whip in hand, as a lion tamer. Everybody knew their role and had his strengths and his weaknesses. Some I could turn my back on and feel confident that I would not be struck with an angry claw nor have my head chewed off; with others, or should I say with one other, I had to keep my eyes open constantly in order to assure that all mayhem did not break out.

It was not like I was demonic and just wanted them to drink my Kool-aid without asking any questions. The best situation for all was when the practice was hitting on all cylinders and running like a finely tuned machine. However, clashes of styles have occasionally caused the engine to misfire; and the root cause generally was traceable back to Brent.

Like déjà vu, Rachel's voice screeched out on the intercom, "David, the food is here. Shall I bring it in now or do you still need some time?" Fortunately, this time the interruption broke into only office small talk, and not one of my recurring fantasies such as a few minutes ago.

She carried in two platters of sandwiches, condiments, and cookies from Epstein's Deli, circled the room taking beverage requests, and asked if we needed anything else. She returned with my Diet Coke and the others' selections so quickly that I was not even able to slather mustard on my corned beef, prior to her reappearance. As was usually the case at these meetings, there appeared to be a sandwich and two cookies missing. That must have been her stipend for carrying out the catering chores.

We always eat first and ask questions later at the monthly meetings. Accordingly, thirty minutes had elapsed and we still had not gotten to the first item on the agenda. Through our casual conversations, I had learned of, but did not care about, the Dolphins' pre-season scrambling to gather a winning squad; how Jesse's son was progressing with his Bar-Mitzvah lessons, rumors that Peter, our young office boy, would be leaving because he does not earn enough, and the clerical staff is in an uproar because they feel our data processing equipment is nearing obsolescence. As usual, maybe one topic tossed around during the informal luncheon foreplay would rise to the top and warrant further consideration. I made a mental note to check out the concerns about our computers with Justin, our I.T. consultant not just wanting to ameliorate the staff, but to ensure that we have the state of the art computers and are poised to be better than our competitors

As the cookie tray made its rounds, my post morning shower battle with the bathroom scale as well as Elaine's comments suggested that I did not really need that macadamia nut pastry. Dessert always precedes and leads into the business portion of the meeting. Although I set the agenda and monitor its execution, the lead for each discussion is handled by the partner most closely involved with the item at hand. Boringly, the meetings always commence with a presentation of financial data which is delivered by me.

Each month, the report is substantially identical, except for the numbers. I could almost be reciting a script, in fact I do. Blah, Blah, Blah, our receivables aggregate $......., of which $........ are past due. I try to get my dig in with, "Brent, most of the delinquencies are made up of your clients. Tighten the reins and get them current." He rarely does. Our payables are $...... and we currently have $...... in the bank. Work-in-process accumulated time is too high, please review and get some interim billings out. Yada, Yada, Yada.

Although subject to changes brought about by unforeseen crises, the next item discussed each month was staff utilization for the upcoming month. Many tasks are predictable, court hearings, discovery, anticipated trial dates, normal recurring compliance services and the like.

"As of today, our team is actively engaged, and we have very little non-chargeable time. There had been no unanticipated surprises and we're very confident that by this time next month we will be in overdrive entrenched in the upcoming unregistered securities trial as well as the initial public offering of Okeechobee County cattle ranchers' common stock."

I alerted the boys that I would be out of the office from Friday returning to the office on Tuesday morning. Each knew me well enough to guess that I would be in the Bahamas, Atlantic City or some other gaming venue. When I informed them that I would be Vegas, I received the predictable recommendations of where to eat and who to see. I thanked them, but I would have little time for such frivolities, I would be at the Black Jack tables.

Saving the subject of Judith Kaplan's promotion for the last matter, I opened the floor for any other pressing issues not already discussed. Ed was the only one to comment and it involved Ms. Kaplan. Serving as the perfect segue, we commenced airing the pro's and cons of inviting her to join the partnership. I, however, made it clear that I wanted to deliberate over this issue carefully and that we would conduct a formal partnership vote during the next month, October's meeting.

Recognizing that we had aired all that had to be aired, I called for an adjournment setting Tuesday, October 5th for our next luncheon. Since I already had a meeting scheduled with Judith and our new Associate, Deborah West, in about an hour, I told the gang that I would inform her that we would reach our decision next month. Within a minute the room was cleared of the top five and shortly thereafter, the office vultures descended upon the conference table scoffing away the remains of Epstein's offerings like they would a prey's carcass.

CHAPTER 3

Bloated from lunch and back at my desk, I was glad that I passed on those cookies, but I should have also taken a pass on the second half sandwich. Happily Elaine was not there to chide me about the overeating. No sweat, she had her surrogate permanently housed in my office. Specifically, hanging on my certificate wall, directly across the room from my work station, is a portrait of my dad. He stands guard over me every day, and right then he was giving me hell for carrying that extra fifteen pounds I have managed to collect since the first of the year by multiple samplings of Epstein's fine array of cured meats.

It seems appropriate at this juncture to discuss another of Epstein's treats, although this one is not edible: It is a coffee mug. Catering to a Jewish clientele, the facility is adorned with cutesy placards of Yiddish Wisdom distinctly posted throughout the eatery as well as coffee mugs imprinted with the same or similar expressions. The message and cup which impresses me on each visit illustrates my feelings towards my dad at various stages of our lives; and I have ever so slightly edited the *YIDDISHA KOP* to read:

Father

4 years:	My Daddy can do anything.
7 years:	My Daddy knows a lot, a whole lot.
12 years:	Oh well, naturally Father doesn't know everything.
14 years:	Father? Hopelessly old fashioned
21 years:	Oh that man is out of date! What did you expect
25 years:	He knows a little bit about it, but not much.
30 years:	I must find out what Dad thinks about it.

35 years: A little patience please. Let's get Dad's meaning first.
50 years: My Dad knew literally everything.
55 years: I wish I could talk it over with Dad once more.

Dan Fogelberg, the late song writer and singer, eulogized his deceased father in his signature song, "........my life has been a poor attempt to imitate the man. I am just a living legacy to the Leader of the Band." I lived my earlier days striving to impress my dad and gain his approval; though he is gone, it is still my quest, but my progress is difficult to assess.

Elaine's good friend, Marjorie, an exceptionally talented artist, painted a portrait of dad shortly after he left us. She must have been truly inspired as her work is the next best thing to actually having him present with me. She captured his smile, the glint in his eyes, the always too long ash on his cigar and so much more. Whenever I have a problem requiring resolution, the painting becomes my Ouija Board; my Magic Eight Ball; and together we logically tackle whatever the world throws my way.

My focus on the painting is interrupted as Judith, soon to become my business partner, entered the office. She is thirty-six both chronologically and dimensionally; blonde, smart and articulate. Her handmaiden, Deborah, our newest and youngest associate, a recent graduate of Florida (Go Gators), is a step behind towing three bankers' boxes of legal documents on a trolley.

The ladies were there to discuss a Form S-1 to be filed with the United States Securities and Exchange Commission relating to Mid-Florida Cattle Consortium, Inc.'s initial public offering of 10 million shares in which they hope to raise $100 million dollars for expansion of their operations. Why I was needed at that meeting was yet to be determined; they certainly could have gotten further into the project before requiring my assistance.

Judith was wearing a sexy, yet professional charcoal pin-striped suit with the skirt not quite covering her knees. Deborah is modeling a smart floral skirt with a lovely pink pastel blouse. They take their seats, and Ms. Kaplan simultaneously removes her jacket and swivels to place it on the back of her chair. In so doing, the slightest glimpse of a black lace bra is revealed between the buttons on her grey blouse.

Ebony lingerie is by far my favorite. Not needing much more catalyst, she mouths "David, are you ready for us?" It was post time and I was off to the races!

What was she thinking phrasing that question that way? With two attractive women in my presence, I am always ready. There it was: The mother load of all fantasies, a threesome! I pushed my chair further into its hangar under my desk so as to hide the anticipated rising evidence. I looked at the clock and noted that it was nearing 3:30 in the afternoon, and I shifted the gears into auto-pilot. Checklist completed, I was about to launch into my second virtual escapade of the day.

That one however was different; there would be others in the room requiring a split screen reflecting both fantasy and reality as events unfolded. Oh to be a fly on the wall to observe both views: Watching me contribute sage advice professionally, while traipsing through the Garden of Eden in my mind. Although I would never partake of that forbidden apple in real life, I took two bites, one for each of my willing playmates and away I went.

Judith was pouring over the prospectus and wondering if the Risk Factor section was adequately documented. She laid out a sampling of other filings displaying how these matters were handled in other documents recently submitted to the SEC. I perused the materials while watching the two ladies remove their first layer of clothing. Deborah's skirt and blouse hit the floor followed quickly by Judith's.

What a life!

The recent co-ed's youth and eagerness to please was immediately evident as she headed south of the border fumbling with my zipper giving her the opportunity to display her considerable oral talents, while her older partner stood close by observing, in a maternal manner. Judith must have been feeling deprived as she watched her kitten take too many laps on the Top Dog. In short order the Green Eyed Monster took aim at the One Eyed Monster and the scene turned into a frenzied cat fight. Each woman vying for my attention and trying to hold on and play with my toy until it was pried away by the other. The ensuing contest ultimately resulted in Deborah retreating for greener pastures, yielding the trophy for her mentor.

She wiggled out of her remaining clothes and hovered above my head she forming another triangle. Her legs straddle my head and at the apex angle was her shaven mons pubis. As she spread her legs, the angle increased and moving the prize closer to my face and providing an unfettered view into that mysterious crevice that all men covet.

"David, I have to use the ladies room."

What?! My mind tried to adjust; Ladies Room, did I need an umbrella? Wait, that was Judith speaking, not Deborah, I was all clear; at least as far as it related to potential monsoons.

She added, "Please review the adequacy of the Related Party Transactions section while I am gone." Is Judith nuts? Scanning down, I noticed that we are already on page 37 of the prospectus. Apparently, we have gotten through more than half of the document with my quasi involvement. I guess that we made some progress on both levels; and my secret journey was still my secret.

"Deborah, do you want a break also" I asked politely.

Her response, "No, I can wait, why don't we carry on?"

I thought, but did not state, *carry on*, indeed. This girl showed a lot or promise. As Judith would be gone for at least five minutes, I decided to return to my Nubian fantasy mate, Deborah.

My quick return to Eden was suddenly thwarted when she added, "Oh David, I love working here. My fiancé works just down the street and my father-in law, to be, has his office on the fourth floor of our building." A fiancé, a father-in-law, oh shit! Game over; the metaphorical buckets of ice cubes and Gatorade were poured over my crotch, only this time, I was the losing coach.

Fortunately, my pants felt dry and a quick glance downward confirmed the same. I gazed up at the clock, 4:15 and then over to dad's portrait. He was laughing his ass off!

Judith re-entered the room just as I concluded that I already had enough. Before she could take her seat, my attention was back on the cattle deal. I dutifully informed her that although I would be out of the office from Friday returning Tuesday, AM, I wanted to get a draft to the client by the close of business on Tuesday. "We should receive the accountant's financial statements and related data no later than Friday." And, as an afterthought, "Oh, with respect to the Related Party Transactions Section, I think you should beef it up a bit." Either I was too esoteric, or these ladies have no sense of humor!

After the documents were gathered and the boxes refilled, the ladies passed the obligatory pleasantries one imparts to a senior colleague prior to taking leave. I suggested that Judith stay behind a moment, causing the slightest of hesitations in Deborah's gait as she pondered why she was excluded from the invitation. Apparently Deborah was too inexperienced to realize that if I held one of them behind for that reason, it would have been her.

I related, "Judith, I wanted to tell you that your promotion was discussed at this afternoon's Partner Meeting and we decided that each of us should take one more month to individually assess the matter. We will reach a final decision during October." Intuitively I believed that the vote would go her way, so I added, "Don't worry, it'll be fine."

"Thanks, David." She paused, and then added, in her smart ass fashion that I have learned to respect and admire, "I have waited this long, I guess I can wait another month for my key to the *MEN'S ROOM!*"

Although it was only 5:07 PM and I usually could be found in my office until 6:30 or later, I was ready to head south for a special evening with my bride. After all, she promised to reward me, more specifically "Make it up to me" for approving her week-end getaway with Susan.

"Rachel, Rachel, are you there," I shouted into the intercom.

"David, David, of course, where the hell do you think I would be?" she replied ignoring the respect that I thought I deserved.

"I am leaving a little early. If Elaine calls, tell her I am on my way".... and expecting her to be waiting at the door with nothing on but a smile. "What's on the calendar tomorrow, do I need to be here early?"

"I do not see anything until lunch with Randall Savage at the Breakers," she replied.

"Thanks, have a great evening. In fact, why don't you get the hell out of here also?"

"Thanks, boss. See you in the morning." Finally, some respect; and all I had to do was give her an early out.

CHAPTER 4

TUESDAY EVENING

On my way to the elevator, I was practically skipping and euphemistically whistling "Zip idée Do Dah, Zip idée Aye" my, oh my, David is getting laid today. Chalk that down as another of those Mars/Venus things. Men have sex; women make love; sex vs. romance. Is that wrong? I met Elaine when we were sixteen and thirteen, respectively, and told my mom after our first date that I was going to marry her. She is still as pretty as she was then; isn't that romantic? And, she has a better shape than any of our friends, with or without cosmetic assistance; more input from Mars.

The door opens on the lower level garage, the cavern housing my car, which is parked within fifteen feet of the elevator. Rank does have its privileges! However, even the General could not avoid the perils and frustrations of I-95 traffic rush hour, which is unquestionably, the worst in the country. Naturally, such was the sentiment felt by every metropolitan commuter about his individual stretch of road between the office and his evening sanctuary. I, however knew that this one is truly the worst. Notwithstanding, I was already allowing myself to think about the SEC and the District of Columbia's Beltway.

I pulled out of the garage trying to decide on which topic would fill my commute; I had Elaine on one shoulder, George Bush and a presidential appointment on the other. The battle lines were set for the drive home. Who would prevail? It really was an easy choice. After all, I am from Mars and thinking only of Elaine.

By the time I reached Lantana, I found myself humming another verse of Zipidee and pondering the upcoming good fortunes that would unfold that evening. The traffic was surprisingly light, but I contemplated that the sex would be heavy. What would she be wearing as she greeted me at the door? If not at the door, where would she be lying in wait?

Passing Delray Beach, I was getting really anxious; it was just another seven or eight miles to paradise. Some might find this strange. After all, we had been married for almost thirty years, raised three children and gone through all the growing pains associated therewith. And yet, there I was, after thousands of sexual couplings with Elaine, so aroused at her promise "to make it up to me."

Exiting on Glades Road west, I will momentarily be in our community, Boca's Floral Lagoon. I made my left on Rhododendron Lane, punched the homing button on my Mercedes to open the gate, made a quick right onto Hibiscus Way and followed the road right into our Azalea Court. Another punch on the adjacent homing device and the garage door sprung into action providing access to our private retreat.

Heart be still! Surely she would be eagerly waiting for me on the other side of the door, stretched out atop the washer and dryer in a fluffy bathrobe subtly concealing her naked body with a rose adorning her eager smile.

What? The only mounds I see in the laundry room are towels piled high; no smiling face, no nakedness, and no rose.

The next logical choice was that she would be provocatively lying on the dining room table with our cornucopia centerpiece appropriately positioned to suggest the treats awaiting me just beyond. Strike two!

Mighty Casey had two strikes and the next pitch would have to be from the kitchen; not necessarily a hub of sensuality, but any port would do in a storm, and the clouds were gathering. I hear her shuffling pots and pans; she really is a fox preparing dinner with only her apron on. Not quite, I notice that she's fully garbed as she gives me a peck on the cheek and instructs me to open a bottle of red wine to accompany our steaks. Some reward, but still a foul tip; I had not struck out just yet.

One would think that after all our years she would have learned that the fastest route to a man's heart is not through his stomach? The more direct route starts a bit lower.

I freed the cork from the bottle, took two glasses in tow, and I found her on our patio readying the grill for its duties. The sun is saying its goodbyes for the day in magical fashion over the lake which forms the border of our property. We moved here from Broward County several years ago primarily to shorten my commute. However, both the floor plan of our new residence and the prerequisite lake, were beyond our expectations making the decision easy.

I do not know when it happened, but we became empty nesters. The kids were gone. Darlene and Lenny had graduated college and, at least for now, have remained in Gainesville and Tampa, respectively. Michael just started his undergraduate days at South Florida. We only experience the prior norm, the household cacophony of wants and needs resulting in a sibling challenge to garner most of their parent's attention, when our offspring returned home for holidays and vacations. The otherwise quiet solace of our evenings provides considerable privacy and intimacy. However, as experienced, at least so far that evening, Elaine did not take full advantage of our environment and ignore some of her inhibitions. I had not quite thrown in the towel. The night was young and after dinner and another bottle of wine, I would work our way over to the Jacuzzi.

While intermittently peering over the lake and back to Elaine's beautiful ass as I marveled her skill at the grill, I heard her report, "Darlene called this afternoon. She's starting to get real serious with Ethan. She suggested that they come home next week-end and that we should go out to dinner with them and his parents."

Are these ladies both nuts? "Not this week-end, we are going away!"

"No, no, not this week-end; next week, and what do you mean we? Only Susan and I are going, I already explained that to you."

What I wanted to say was, you also said you would make it up to me, I'm waiting. However, what I said was, "Oh, just after you called, Doc and I had a conversation and I suggested that with you out of town, perhaps we could go to Las Vegas for the week-end. He's checking with

21

Maggie." I think that came off seamlessly. Now a quick change of pace, "isn't the sunset marvelous tonight?"

"That was real smooth, David, but I guess you deserve a boy's getaway also. I'll be shocked if Maggie lets him go."

How charitable! He would be shocked if she let me go assuming the tables were reversed. "Thanks, it will be good for both of us. Are the steaks done yet? I am horny, I mean hungry."

I went inside and scoffed up her table settings and re-arranged the scene to the patio table. I so prefer eating *al fresco*. I informed her that I would finish the steaks and that she should finish up things inside. In conjunction with these new responsibilities, I lit a few candles and flipped on the Jacuzzi, attempting to create a romantic scene. Elaine returned to the kitchen to finalize the dinner accompaniments, potatoes and asparagus; why not oysters?

"These steaks are great, where did you get them?" I served up as dinner question number one.

"Costco, of course. Don't you want to talk about Darlene's call?"

"I guess it's inevitable that she will fall in love and get married one of these days. Ethan seemed like a nice enough jerk based on the two times that we met him." I had called all the males that Darlene brought home since high school, Jerk. Another entry for our *Ode to the Jewish Husband*, no guy would ever be good enough for my little girl. "I hope she now understands why I insisted that she stay within the state for her education." Such was my practical prophesy; kids will meet their mates while away at college and the odds of having a future Floridian as our in-law improves if he or she is selected from a local school.

She cautiously responds, "Let's not rush things."

"You brought up the topic; I'm already in the Jacuzzi having sex."

"You are such a jerk."

Me a jerk! I thought Ethan was the jerk. I had better change the subject, "These steaks are great. Where did you get them?" Shortly thereafter, I found out who won the jerk contest between me and Ethan. Take a guess.

The steaks were so good than we cleared our plates before I could make my third inquiry about Costco. In deference to my devilish ulterior motives, I cleaned the table and loaded the dishwasher. One will find this maneuver and similar other alternatives discussed under the caption, <u>Things to do if you want to have sex</u> in the aforementioned *Ode to the Jewish Husband.*

Elaine finally got the message and went into the house to change into a bathing suit. Gee, what an intuitive women. After all, my hints were extremely subtle. I put on a romantic CD, grabbed two glasses and another bottle of wine and skipped over to the spa, got undressed, gave a friendly good evening wave to Steven, next door as he lowered his binoculars purchased in the Bahamas on our last vacation together, and eased to the swirling waters. I wondered why he needed binoculars. Now I knew!

I guess the wine was making me a bit silly. It must have been the wine. What else would explain not discussing the article I read earlier relating to my possible appointment to the Securities and Exchange Commission during dinner? Reflecting further on the subject, I wondered if that was the reason Randall Savage, Chairman of Palm Beach County Republican Committee, arranged our luncheon tomorrow. I could not think of another reason. It appeared that I might need to buy a few heavier suits for the cooler days ahead in Washington.

As I watched Elaine exiting our bedroom door the patio candles behind her created a magnificent silhouette as she made her way towards the Jacuzzi. I was blessed with good fortune by winning her hand in matrimony. I truly caught the gold ring. With all my moaning and groaning, I know what I have, and she is wonderful. However, did she have to be wearing a damned bathing suit?

I touched Elaine's beautiful face and kissed her succulent lips while struggling to remove her bikini top. I guess I still had not mastered that act that befuddles males, unfastening a bra in one fluid motion. Once again she called me a jerk, but this time it was with affection as she facilitated the process by freeing herself of both pieces of cotton. So much for the SEC!

We kissed and probed each other's bodies as though we were still in high school. Notwithstanding the fact that we have been at it for so many years, I love sex, oh, oh, making love, with Elaine. The logical half of my brain was still in Mars and appreciative of the chemicals in the spa which would neutralize any deposits we left in the water. We shared a few post coital kisses and hugging until the CD ended signaling our exit to the shower.

I was the first in the bathroom, lighting candles to set a more welcoming atmosphere. As Elaine entered the room clearly noticing the romantic ambience and once again indicated what a jerk I was as she proffered a passionate kiss and joined me in the shower. I already forgot my earlier disappointment entering the laundry room followed by the sad visit to the dining room. Bingo, round two!

Since the requisite thirty minutes had not yet elapsed allowing my body to relax and assume its pre-Jacuzzi functionality, I wisely chose to kiss Elaine romantically while conveying my love for her; all the while keeping one eye on the clock hanging above that dreaded scale. Confirmed by the timepiece, the symbolic half-hour egg timer went off as did the water jets in our shower.

Trying to keep drying and powdering time to a minimum, I lifted her off her feet and whisked her off to the bed. Not to overwork my expressions of glee over her appearance and physique, I would surely have thrown my back out carrying too much weight and my sexual desires would have been diminished, if she were anyone but Elaine.

The combination of alcohol and coming up to bat a second time provided for a longer more enhanced sensual experience. Thank you Dionysius, the Greco-Roman God of Wine! All nonsense aside, we do love each other and could not be happier with our respective choices of life partners. She is the love of my life. After much huffing and puffing, the crescendo is reached. Both of us retreat to the north and south sides of our bed to catch our breath.

I whispered, "Give me thirty minutes….forty-five at most."

For the last time that evening, she sensually responded, "You are such a jerk!"

Two minutes later, we were both asleep.

CHAPTER 5

WEDNESDAY MORNING

I awoke euphemistically with the roosters. It was 6:00 A.M, Wednesday, and the clock radio alarm did its job, as requested, waking me to Reba McEntire singing *The Greatest Man I Never Knew.* Since this song has a significant meaning in my relationship with my father, I listened until its heart wrenching ending. Predictably, I then switched from radio to television to get a weather and traffic update, learning that I could expect an easy commute to the office that morning. As was the case last night, the morning flow should also be light.

As the steaming jets of my shower cascaded down my back relaxing every muscle, my smile developed into a full grin; my face reflected the pleasures of last evening's delights. What a way to start the day, Reba, a promised easy commute, and fond visions of my previous evening with Elaine.

I turned off the water was grabbing a towel when she strolled into the bathroom and greeted me with a "Good morning tiger."

Toweling myself dry, I replied, "Look who's talking? Good morning sweetheart."

Even as she wakes up, without having the opportunity to apply her make up, she still looks beautiful, at least ten years younger than her age. That was the only explanation as to why I completely forgot to discuss my noon luncheon with Randall Savage during our dinner conversation last evening. My mind was on much more important matters; my libido was in overdrive and prurient visions superseded any thoughts of Washington and the SEC.

I am not a complete cad. Elaine and I had discussed this topic in varying degrees of intensity over the past month. Such ponderings were predicated on the occasional hints and innuendos that arose and their perceived veracity. None the less, Elaine was unaware that I would be meeting with Savage that day and that the meeting might signal that the process would be taking a giant step towards reality.

She recognized my enthusiasm and walked with me into the kitchen. I popped a bagel in the toaster, poured ten ounces of java into my travel mug and worked on the morning Jumble until I heard the bell indicating the completion of toasting and warning that my bagel halves would be sprung skyward. Oh shit, I was supposed to stop at Target yesterday in order to pick up a more reliable unit. Too bad, that day I would dine on the air cooled variety. I added two slices of American cheese to my feast and grabbed a napkin before kissing Elaine good-bye. "Have a great day, sweetheart, I love you."

"Knock him dead at lunch. I can't wait to flit between here and D.C. I am so proud of you."

What a woman! I do live a charmed life.

Office bound, not quite singing Zip idée Do Dah, but quite pleased that Channel 3's Eye over Palm Beach was correct. I found I-95 moving along nicely. I just completed my merge into the northbound flow when my cell phone signaled an incoming call. I anticipated it being Doc, but it was Lenny, my eldest son. As it was only 7:15 AM, I thought, this could not be good; he is usually not even awake at this hour. Oh wait, he started his new job with that mutual fund company, of course he would be up already. He may even have been at his desk.

"Hi Pops," he greets.

Good, it is the casual greeting. This generally equates, on a monetary scale, to only hundreds as compared to the more serious salutation, which often reaches into the thousands of dollars. "Lenny, I am surprised to hear from you so early in the morning. What's cooking?" I asked while chewing away on my bagel.

After a brief exchange, his tone and cadence seemed to suddenly switch gears. He must have rehearsed his pitch. The presentation lasted thirty seconds without his taking a breath. "Naturally, I enjoy talking to you, but…" *Here it comes*, "……wardrobe is still college stuff and I'll need a few suits, sports jackets for the new job, you know.………If OK, I will charge the new threads on my emergency credit card. Isn't this an emergency? Thanks Pops. Gotta go ….Love ya, same to Mom."

It seemed like only yesterday ago that Lenny headed west for Tampa. His college days were apparently the best five or six years of his life, as I was sure Michael's would be. He finished the job, earning a degree in business and was now starting his career. I so missed our "guy time." Over the years, we had been to every sporting venue in the tri county area. Not so much because I was huge fan, we went because Lenny was and still is a sports fanatic. No difference if it was the Dolphins, the Marlins, the Heat, the Panthers or the Miami Grand Prix; he loves sports. In his earlier years, his passion was professional wrestling. We would continually debate whether it is an actual professional sport or staged entertainment. Where has the time gone?

Truth be told, Lenny is the most sensitive and loving of our children. Our mid-week evening conversations are much more meaningful than the one just concluded. We catch up on the week just past and plans for the one upcoming. We share family news and always close our calls with mutual expressions of love. The Wednesday night call was initiated during his college days by Elaine and has endured post graduation; a parental reward to see your kid still wants to be connected.

The Okeechobee Boulevard exit is a line of demarcation in the commute. Its winding drive along the gorgeous Intercoastal Waterway which leads directly into our in-building parking garage signaling that the business day is about to begin. The morning had, thus far, demonstrated the promise of a blossoming into splendid day.

The smartly designed gold-plated AI&S signage greets the opening elevator door on the seventeenth floor. I often reminisce over my earlier offices from the sole practitioner days, through my affiliation with Immerson and the current professionally decorated suite; full of pride I still get a kick out of the package that I have put together. I continued my proud strut into the office.

"Good morning, Brent" He must be purposely trying to alter my mood. Once again he had demonstrated his one-upmanship by arriving at the office earlier than me. What a child; him or me?

"Hey David, heading out to Vegas?" he rubs in, loud enough for the people in Dade County to hear.

"Bet on it," I respond metaphorically.

Needing to upstage, he re-responds, "Buena suerte" drawing the Spanish he learned during his days living in Miami.

Such was indicative of our recent conversations: A short staccato of barbs and quick retorts. It was really strange when you consider how close we once were. He knew that his extramarital affair really irked me. How could he show Jennifer so little respect and how would he explain it to his son, Mitchell, if it ever leaked out? His outside relationship should have been none of my business, but it became primary as to how I looked at him.

His behavior constantly made me wonder if he would screw me also. We had become more and more distant and it appeared he availed himself of any opportunity that presented itself to outdo or embarrass me. It certainly was not healthy to our personal relationship nor was it good for the business end of things either. I would have to address that at a later date. However, I had more important fish to fry over the coming days, it would have to wait at least until my return from Vegas.

What a surprise, Rachel has not arrived yet. The published business hours commenced at 9:00 AM. However, most of the team was at their desks within minutes of 8:00. Unless I begged her for an early start the night before, she rarely got in before 9:15. And, she always had an endless supply of reasons explaining away her tardiness. Rachel had been with me for almost a decade, kept a tight rein over my activities, efficiently got our work done, and continues to be an effective business adjunct. After all, she is like family.

So much like family, in fact, I usually have to get my own coffee. At least she ensured that we have that dark espresso roast blend. Most mornings required the caffeine jolt of two cups of the stuff in order to get going. However, everything had been meshing together so nicely that I felt as though all I wanted was decaffeinated that morning. Not a chance. How could anyone drink that swill?

The computer booted-up into my e-mail inbox. Reviewing the messages, I found that it is difficult to avoid those pesky Viagra advertisements. My left brain asks would I ever need that stuff, and if so, when? My right brain, in full concert with my penis responded, mind your own business, we are doing fine. In fact, last night we went into over-time.

The first valid e-mail, after three straight from marketers of the Blue Wonder drug was from Doc, and it is time stamped 3:14 AM

It must be bad news or he would have waited and called. The content was bad, as he indicated that he could not accompany me to L.V. However, it was not terrible. He threw his back out last evening planned to see his buddy, the chiropractor, first thing that morning. That made the third time he had sustained some malady or illness resulting in a no-show for our gaming outing.

That was just great! When would we have another golden opportunity like that one? Oh well, as much as I hated to do so, I decided to go by myself. "Rachel, get me Corey Alexander on the phone." What was I thinking? It was only 9:12 AM and Rachel still had three minutes on her pass. She is so much like family that I had to dial my own phone.

"Corey, hi how are you? This is David Atlas. Can you set me up at Paris, I will get in Friday late afternoon, out Monday about 9:00 PM?"

He asked his usual questions about the amount of my anticipated table action. I responded the same way as always, "Nah, I will be playing about the same level as last time. If that is not fully acceptable to them for a comp, see what you can do with free room only."

Now you know the truth. Although I love visiting casinos around the world, I do not wager sufficiently to motivate the casino to provide a full comp. I am not a whale!

He assured me that he would do his best and added "Give me a call later today or tomorrow and I will let you know what they say."

Trying, but not succeeding, to be cool, I added, "Later dude."

My request was completed and, even though he expressed some concern, he had never let me down before and I felt confident that I would have a free room once I got to Vegas.

"Rachel, are you here yet?" I ponder into the intercom.

"Of course I am here, who do you think you are talking to? I have been here for almost an hour, but I saw your phone line was in use and did not want to disturb you."

Well, that explains her absence over the past two minutes. Nice try Rachel, however she is so much like family, I just accept it. Moving on, I requested, "Can you please bring me a cup of coffee?"

She replied, "No, I am busy, get it yourself!"

While I sipped my self-retrieved cup of Joe, I recounted the last hour. Things were going along wonderfully until I got that e-mail from Doc. I have got Ms. Attitude up front and Doc bent like a Pretzel to deal with, in the wings. I thought I would just sequester myself for the remainder of the morning and prepare for the pending session with Randall Savage. I pulled out a folder containing news clippings discussing Randall, his acquaintances, his education, his family, etc. I suspect that you get the picture: I wanted to be prepared when we dove into our shrimp cocktails.

It would be hard for anybody in Florida to not know who he was. However, I had never met Randall Savage personally. That is why I thought it strange when he invited me to lunch. At first I believed it had to do with legal representation, but I had since become convinced that the luncheon would begin our courting dance to see if I would truly become the man he pitched to Jeb Bush.

Having read all the articles and making notes, a damn good job I might add, I saw that we had a lot in common; not really. He cut his teeth in Miami real estate during the seventies and eighties; I went to school for two years at the University of Miami. He is a life-long dyed in the wool Republican; I am a Registered Independent, but historically voted Blue more often than Red. He knows every politician in the state; I had lunch with my state representative once. He is a male; I am a male. This was truly a match made in heaven.

It was during Savage's Miami days of wheeling and dealing in commercial real estate that he met Jeb. Prior to ascending to the gubernatorial seat, Bush arranged many of Miami's most lucrative real estate transactions. My client, Cuban born, Carlos Rodriguez was on either end of many of those. In addition, Carlos owned many entities and our firm was successful in pooling all of them together and guiding them through the largest consolidated common stock offering in the state's history. Interesting, another layer of the onion was peeled and I had almost drilled down to the six degrees of separation inexorably drawing us together.

Carlos always called me his Jewish son and I likewise, was quite fond of him. His attribute to which I most closely related was his strong commitment to his family. He loved his wife viewing her as his life soulmate and involved her in all matters of his being. He also recognized the similarity within my family life. This feeling of simpatico was the nucleus and glue of our relationship.

Often, life gets in the way. I have not had much contact with him in recent years. My kids, Darlene and Lenny, were off to college, and in Michael's case, high school; his boys were taking over the family business. Fortunately for Carlos, he had systematically reduced his holdings in the company converting the equity to hard cash. After years away from active participation in corporate affairs, he was worth zillions and his former company was nearing bankruptcy. Apparently his looking out for me was his way of saying gracias.

No Carlos, Gracias to you! He may be my Cuban father, but that was only by proxy. If he was able to make this thing with Bush and the SEC happen he would have made my Jewish father very proud. Albeit, posthumously! It goes to show that the world is indeed small; a Cuban exiled from Havana can take care of a Jew exiled from Brooklyn.

For the first time that day, I looked up at Dad's portrait. I sensed his pride and complete concurrence with my actions of the morning. That type of communion with his painting always prompted the same reaction; he died too young and I was cheated out of his counsel, friendship, and wisdom way before I should have.

Anne Sexton wrote "it doesn't matter who my father was; it matters who I remember he was."

William Atlas, my dad was also known as honey, Dad, Pops, Uncle Willie or Grandpa Bull, depending on whether you were talking to my mother, my older sister Florence, my kid brother Donald, my countless cousins, or Florence's children, respectively. He was born in 1917, lived through the Great Depression, served in the Philippines during WWII, and came home choosing printing and graphics as his profession. He died of lung cancer before his sixty-seventh birthday.

He and Mom married and popped out three kids in approximate three year intervals, after taking a few for getting to know each other. I was the second of three, but spared of the customary problems associated with the being in the middle; I was the normal one. Of course, I am also the judge! Oh wait, it is going to be a Commissioner, not a judge.

At the time, I thought life was great. We had a television, Dad took me to Dodger games, we went away every summer, and we ate Chinese food every Sunday. The Atlas brood moved from Brooklyn to the suburbs of Long Island just after my eleventh birthday. I did harbor a lot of resentment; how could I live without Miss Fox? She was soon forgotten in exchange for the swimming pools that Levittown offered. I did not know it then, but she would return to my life as a frequent visitor when I needed a pick-me-up.

As I became more sophisticated, I realized how stretched the family finances really were. Retracing the various home moves that we experienced, it became apparent that each coincided with the family's need for money. I was laden with a heavy dose of Jewish guilt as Mom and Dad insisted on paying for my college education. Fortunately, Dad's sister found me a scholarship for my final two years. Accordingly, I only drained the family's piggy bank for two years. Thereafter, Florence and Donald picked up the slack and ensured our parents' continuing life of struggling to maintain financial equilibrium.

Once again, Rachel, broke the mood, "David, did you forget your luncheon? You had better get going; you are scheduled to be there in ten minutes." Where was she ten minutes ago when she should have reminded me? No need to ask, she had her excuse all queued up.

"Thanks R, I am on my way."

I have already presented my recurring elevator/automobile drill; no need to be redundant. Although the scenery between the office and the Breakers Resort is beautiful, I have come to take it for granted. My route takes me over the Intercoastal Bridge and one mile up the beach. My Navigation System suggests that I should be there in six minutes. It is amazing: A Japanese woman's voice, in a German car, instructed me, a Jewish man, to take the next left on an American road, Route A1A. We live in a global world and it is getting smaller everyday.

CHAPTER 6

WEDNESDAY AFTERNOON

Of the iconic landmarks in Palm Beach, the Breakers is at the top. It is only a short drive up the beach; a strip sporting many mansions of indescribable opulence. The occasional gaps between residences offer spectacular vistas of the Atlantic Ocean. A quick right hand turn leads into the quarter mile, well manicured palm tree lined driveway. The GPS indicated that I had arrived at my destination. This was confirmed as Raymond, the next car valet, who welcomed me to the Breakers and zoomed away to my parking spot leaving two feet of rubber on the red stone pavers.

Visitors are impressed by an arched ceiling, reminiscent of European architecture with crystal chandeliers of the same genre spaced at appropriate intervals; retail shops to the right, restaurant and beach access to the left. It was prearranged that I would meet Savage in the Ocean Grill. Depending on the table assigned to us, we would either have a view of the fabled tenth hole, with its sand trap guarded green, or waves crashing ashore on a pristine white sanded beach. My preference was the latter; I got the former.

Notwithstanding my late departure from the office, I arrived at our table in time to see a golfer shoot five pounds of sand twenty feet into the air as he attempted to move his ball the five yards between him and the hole. Wouldn't lunch be more enjoyable watching sun-tanned-oiled tourists soaking in Florida's best?

I greeted Randall within a minute of the designated hour. It is strange how these things go. Although we had never met, we both recognized each other immediately. I must confess it was easier for me, as his picture appeared regularly in the Post. I suspected that he had been able to spot me as a result of his probable background research into my past. After all, he did not just pick my name out of the phone book!

"David, I am glad we finally have this opportunity to meet," was Savage's opening gambit.

"I was surprised when you called, and it is truly a pleasure to meet you," was my counter.

"Sorry, they did not have a table overlooking the beach. Some of the tourist bikinis that you see here leave little to the imagination. This table isn't too shabby, I love golf and the tenth is my favorite hole. Do you play?"

Making a mental note to get more involved with the game, I replied, "I played often when I was in high school and college, but not so much since. I would have preferred a beachside table also."

I began to wonder how long this interminable banter was going to continue. He left golf and immediately dove into another of my favorite topics, the Dolphins, "The 'Fins are opening their season this Saturday against the Titans. Are you going to the game?"

"No, Saturday is September 11th and although three years have elapsed, I still get very reflective on the anniversary, as I lost four close friends in the attacks." Yeah real reflective; I would be reflecting at the tables of the Paris Casino. I felt lousy about using attacks as a reason, I should have been more truthful and just told him the truth that I was not a big fan. Nonsense, I had to get used to fibbing. I was going to Washington.

"It is hard to believe that three years have passed. Sorry to hear about your loss."

Patricia, our server, introduced herself and welcomed us to the Breakers. She must have been trained by the same people as Raymond. She then inquired if we would like to order a beverage. Without a second passing Randall ordered a double Vodka martini. How would it look if the next commissioner of the SEC drank alcohol at lunch? Recognizing that I would need to be focused, if he ever got around to the reason for the luncheon, I ordered an iced tea.

He must be a ventriloquist. In one gulp he drained half the glass and simultaneously without removing the drink from his mouth or moving his lips, ordered another. Savage was so adept at this maneuver that Patricia heard and acknowledged his request even though she was a good thirty feet from the table. My guess was that he had performed such feat before, probably daily, or more often.

While his radar was scanning for her return, he commenced the business portion of the meeting, "It appears that you and I have a mutual friend, a very dear friend, Carlos Rodriguez."

Feigning surprise, I replied "I have not seen much of Carlos recently. However, there was a time when we were very close. He helped me through a tough patch of time when my dad passed away. He even assumed the honorary position of my Cuban father. I must call him. How is he doing?"

Randall chronicled the past decade of Carlos' life concluding with the news that, theretofore unknown to me, he had recently been diagnosed with bone cancer. Further, he indicated that Rodriguez wanted desperately to reward me for the sincere friendship and wise professional counsel we shared over the years; and wanted this accomplished before he died.

"He is a tough cookie; he will put up a good fight. I am going to call him this afternoon."

"Over the past month, he has spoken to me about an appropriate gesture. I am sure that you have heard or read about the rumors related to you and the vacancy on the SEC. Carlos and I have commenced a full court press on Governor Bush to present your name to his brother, W. to appoint you for the job. Are you ready to do some part-time commuting to Washington?"

"I am flattered! Naturally, I have heard bits and pieces, but it is great to hear it officially from the horse's mouth." Or was it the horse's ass?

As the horse's mouth ordered his third martini, he slurred "Jeb is currently on his way to D.C. for a family gathering with his siblings and parents. He is going to call me when he lands. Before he meets with his brother and moves us closer to the goal line, he wants me to get your concurrence to go ahead with the process."

"Once again, I am truly flattered and yes, I would be pleased to accept this honor; of course, with the Advise and Consent of Congress."

He was slow starting the dialogue, but ultimately got it out fast and efficiently. I was wondering if he was going to order yet another cocktail. The question was soon answered when he suggested that we skip lunch as he had already consumed too many calories. In exchange for my passing up on lunch, he offered, "We will get together next week either here, in Tallahassee, or in Washington and we'll have a better meal there."

Hopefully more solid, "That's a great idea, I am not really hungry." I was starving. "See you next week; let me know where and when."

Our server returned, not sure whether she would be making another trip to the bar or a detour to the kitchen to place our order. Since I already knew the answer, my question was whether her facial expression would be relief or disappointment when Savage requested a check, instead. I am also not sure whether he is generous tipper or just a generous drunk. He left a twenty dollar gratuity on a thirty-seven dollar tab. There was no ambiguity in Patricia's next facial expression.

"David, I am glad that we finally met each other. It will be good to have another local boy in Washington. I will let you know what is going on as soon as I know. See you next week."

Although I was walking through the corridors of the Breakers, I pictured myself leaving the restaurant at the Hay-Adams Hotel in D.C. Jeb's plane had not touched down yet, his brother probably did not know who David Atlas was, and I was already counting my Washington chickens before hatching. I handed my chit to Jorge, who had my car available before I finished counting. I suspect Randall's valet had a bigger smile than Jorge's; I only gave him $5.00. He added, "Have a nice day and I hope that you enjoyed your visit to the Breakers."

Heading back to the office, I noticed the upcoming yellow arches of McDonalds. It was as though I was being hypnotized and after all, I Deserved a Break Today; I pulled into the lot and navigated my way to the Drive-Thru lane. There were two cars in front of me, which would usually provide adequate time to follow-up with Corey about my arrangements at Paris, Las Vegas. I dialed his number and he answered after four rings. I said, "Hi Corey, David Atlas here."

"Hello David, I am on the other line. Hold for a sec." He answered switching me over to his office's music-on-hold without waiting for my acceptance of his request. I hate being placed on hold and Heavy Metal is hardly the appropriate choice to while away one's caller's time; most people would prefer calming tones when being inconsiderately being placed on hold for a *second*. Certainly more than the second; in fact four minutes had elapsed when the music broke away into "Sorry, I thought my guy was winding down when you called."

Simultaneously with his return, an almost understandable voice coming through the crackly speaker, "Would you like to have a Big Mac today?"

Notwithstanding who I was on the phone with, it was embarrassing. At the first squeak of the speaker, I immediately sought and pushed the mute button on my cell phone, hoping the Corey would not be aware of my choice of luncheon cuisine. I told the pesky speaker, please hold on. Ronald complied and I spoke into the phone "Corey, I have an incoming call that I need to take. I will get back to you in a few minutes."

"O.K. David, speak to you later....Get fries with that." What a clown! He should apply for Ronald's job.

I ordered a two burger combo lunch intending to dine in my vehicle en route to the office. Retrieving the sack from the clerk, I exited the parking lot and noticed a huge red and white Target staring at me. Good husband that I am, I found a space close to the store, parked my vehicle, swallowed the two burgers in four bites, and began my search for the perfect toaster.

To paraphrase Groucho Marx, "I've had a perfectly wonderful afternoon, but this wasn't it."

CHAPTER 7

It was 2:00 PM when I stepped into the elevator heading up hoping that it was an express car; I needed my Rolaids fiercely. My stomach was on fire! What was wrong with that picture? I had planned on tasty lunch at a fancy resort, but wound up at the last resort for lunch. Ah, but Elaine would be pleased that I remembered her new appliance.

Rifling through my desk, I found my tube of relief, Rolaids. An orange antacid, my favorite was one of only two left. I decided to ingest the yellow one first knowing that I would need at least two. Rapidly chewing the first to create smaller pieces in order to enhance its expediency, I left Mr. Orange to finish the job. Mission accomplished and my stomach felt wonderful as though I had only eaten a bowl of oatmeal for lunch. Relieved, I jotted down the requisite phone calls to be made and tasks to be accomplished for the remainder of the day.

At the top of the list was Elaine. Which should I call first, Speed Dial #1 or #2, home or her cellular phone? Good, I had an exercise in logic to start my afternoon. It was 2:00 PM on a Wednesday. I reasoned, no, Mahjong is Thursday afternoons. Did she tell me she that was going to playing golf in the afternoon? Evaluating the clues and relying on my knowing the woman, I called the house. She answered, confirming that she was not golfing, but goofing.

My opening greeting was, "Hi babe, what's cooking?" What did I tell you? Same opening as always, I lack nearly all originality.

"Hi sweetheart, how did your luncheon go?" she queries with a curious tone.

"Randall Savage is an ass. He drank his lunch, three martinis, as I sipped on a single iced tea. He ultimately confirmed the rumors and indicated that he thinks it's already a done deal."

"Are you happy?" Now, she asks? What is wrong with this woman, didn't she have ample time to serve up that question?

"Of course, I am happy. This is quite an accomplishment." Was I happy? "It's not the Supreme Court, but it's the top of the pyramid for a securities attorney."

"How much time will really be required to be in D.C. as compared to home?" Now, she asks? What is wrong with this woman, didn't she have ample time to serve up that question? This morning, she could not wait to "flit" between here and there, and now, she made it sound like Washington and Hell were synonymous.

Trying to allay her apprehension, I reiterated, "We have already discussed this over and over, it's not really a full-time position; much of the work can be done here in Florida."

The truth was that I did not fully understand what my new responsibilities would entail other than being present whenever the Commission convened to create and monitor adherence to policy. Its composition is a five person body and the incoming candidate must have a political party affiliation other than the previous member selected. The last Commissioner appointed was a Republican and notwithstanding the President being the leader of the GOP, he was legally forced to select a Democrat or Independent candidate.

I went on with, "Savage said that I would meet with the Governor and/or the President next week. Perhaps even at the White House. If the meeting is set in Tallahassee, I will go alone; if in Washington, I want you to come along and we will stay a few extra days to scope things out."

Her enthusiastically stirring congratulations were, "O.K., I guess. I'll see you later. What time are you coming home?" If one looked up the expression, "I guess" (when spoken by a women) in the *Ode to the Jewish Husband,* he would find the translation - such would be her choice only if there is no other possible alternative. The same phrase spoken by a male is usually given from a squatted position after he has ducked trying to avoid flying objects.

Since she set the mood, my near boring response was, "I'll be home at the usual time." I added, "Hey, I purchased the new toaster."

Click!

Switching females, "Rachel, are you there?"

Her way too familiar response was, "If it's not 5:30, I am here. **What?**"

"Did you get me the flight data that I requested?"

Yet another dose of sarcasm, "Did you look at your e-mail?"

I reflexively opened my e-mail and scanned the flight information which was quite satisfactory. I would have plenty of time to deliver Elaine to Susan's and board my plane at 1:00 PM; landing at McCarren International around 3:15 PM, local time. Not being in the mood for a full scale sparring match with Rachel, I simply requested that she ask Deborah, our new associate, to research the SEC, and build a background file for me to read on the plane, this week-end.

Next, I returned the return call to my Casino Host, Corey Alexander, being such a busy guy, I was surprised that he answered on the first ring and I said, "Hi Corey this is David......David Atlas." This guy apparently has a memory like a sieve; I just spoke to him this morning and he could not associate David with Atlas unless I gave him the added input.

"Sorry Dave, it has been a hectic morning. I was able to get you a room comp, but the airfare and meals are on you. You will have to build-up your action before they will pony up more bucks."

This guy has been giving me the same spiel for six years. The wondrous feat that he accomplished for this trip was identical to that which he had done on every previous request. I had never met the man face-to-face, and had no intention to ever do so. He was just a voice on the phone. However, this time I intended to heed his advice and step up the betting, not to get out of hand, but increase my averages to the next level. Perhaps, if I lost a couple of extra thousand dollars, the hotel would pick up a meal or two.

Next call; I reached his voice mail, and I recorded, "Hi Doc. Hope that you're feeling better. A bad back is a real bitch and I know your pain must be terrible; especially if you are going to Todd for treatment." Todd, his neighbor, is a Chiropractor and Doc had to be in a big hurt before having his bones crunched. "I have decided to head west anyway.

It would have been great to have our first Vegas sojourn, but we'll do it some other time. If things improve on your end, give me a call and I'll give you the flight info."

Next call; "Rachel, book the flights included in your e-mail."

"I did it already. Don't you read your e-mail?"

I added, "Excuse me for doubting your efficiency. Can you get me a cup of coffee?" Hopefully that would be her last dose of sarcasm for the day.

"No!"

Apparently, it was not.

I wanted the coffee as I pondered my call to Carlos. I pensively recalled the many cups of *café Cubano* we shared through the years in his Brickell office overlooking Biscayne Bay, the countless eateries along *Calle Ocho* or his residence in Coral Gables. And, now, like my father, he was being consumed by that dreaded disease, cancer.

Rachel has this uncanny intuition to react when I do really require her services; she entered the room with a large mug and a supplemental carafe of black coffee. Showing my sincere appreciation, I said, "Thanks, R."

Next call: and perhaps the most important one of the day, was to Carlos Rodriguez. I spoke into the phone, "Hello Carlos, David. I must apologize for not calling sooner, but I just (almost) had lunch with Randall Savage and learned of your illness. I wish I had learned of it sooner to be with you. How are Juana and the boys? Is there anything I can do for you?" I asked running out of the necessary opening remarks.

"No, David you have done quite enough for me already," was his generous response. "Everyone is holding up nicely, at least for the time being."

"Carlos, I wish this was under different circumstances, but thank you so much for your efforts with the Governor and Randall Savage."

"*De nada, mi amigo*. I hope that I have not overstepped our friendship without discussing this with you first. I do want to read about your appointment in the Miami Herald before I go."

What could I say? "Thank you so much, but you're not going anywhere. You must know that I will think of both of my fathers if, and when I assume my new responsibilities."

"What do you mean if? Jeb owes me, his brother owes him and you are as good as in." was his pure Cuban logic.

Rodriguez was a self made man. His family had plenty of money in Cuba, but that all belonged to Fidel as he scurried out of Havana for the promise of the American Dream in Miami. He left his entire family, except for a brother who joined him on their quest for freedom. Carlos' work ethic and common sense were keen and took him up the ladder of success in rapid fashion.

He always longed for Castro's demise which would enable the return to his homeland. However, time marched on, his parents passed away and his visions of his Cuba tarnished as he earned wealth and fame in Florida. The Bay of Pigs fiasco forced him and his fellow Cubans to hate the Democrats and that distrust, as well as his fortunes, grew over the years as did his power within the Republican Machine.

I concluded, "Carlos, listen, I am going out of town this week-end. Elaine and I will come down to see you next week. Take care of yourself. See you then."

He concluded, "Have a good time in Vegas." How did he know? "*Te amo, mi hijo,*" I love you, my son.

Why are the Cubans such loving people?

Carlos is just about the same age as Dad would have been, had he survived. Yet, his and Dad's American culture of their generation was quite different when comparing how love was demonstrated. Carlos was fluid and giving in his expressions, "*te amo, mi hijo.*" Dad's was much more subdued.

I think back to Reba McEntire waking me up this morning with her "The greatest words I never heard, I guess I'll never hear. The man I thought could never die, has been dead almost a year. He was good at business, but there was business left to do. He never said he loved me, guess he thought I knew."

I lost my father twenty years ago, almost nine months to the day after he was diagnosed with inoperable lung cancer. Our relationship could not have been closer except for the chasm of love expressed by Reba.

It was usually the other way around, but in our case, the parent resided in New York and it was the son who lived in Florida. Air travel obviated the geographic gap; I travelled up to Long Island every other week-end during those miserable months. My primary mission on each trip was to tell him how much I loved him and to finally receive the reciprocal reward. Each Sunday evening's return flight, until the last during his life, was marked with tears in the window as I wondered why this could not be accomplished.

It was during the trip that turned out to be our last visit, three days before he passed, that I summoned the strength and courage to tell him how I felt and, in turn, I experienced a side of him that I only assumed existed. We shared our love for each other. I always knew that he loved me, but I finally heard it. That exchange was one of the most profound in my life and explains my affinity to Fogelberg's "…. I thank you for the kindness and, times that you got tough, and, papa, I don't think I said I love you near enough."

Most fortunately, my generation did not inherit that trait from our parents. From my children's infant days throughout their lives I have openly conveyed my love for each of them through both words and deeds. And, during their teen years, I described my relationship with Dad and the difficulties we both had relative to being able to express love. They only have the faintest of memories of him. What a loss for all.

Aside from the emotional roller coaster I was personally experiencing at that time, our firm was embroiled in a legal mess. Our largest client was under investigation by the state of Florida for fraudulent business practices. As events evolved, he was ultimately indicted and thereafter was sued in several civil actions seeking recovery of funds.

Dad picked one hell of a time to make his exit. I needed his logical wisdom to guide me through this malaise and although comforting, his portrait could only go so far.

CHAPTER 8

Unfortunately, we cannot erase time and yet avoid dealing with the consequences of prior events.

Yes, 1984 was a bleak year; one which I wish never occurred. During that stressful time of my bi-weekly commutes to Long Island, I was introduced to Barry Vincent, who ultimately became a client of, the then, Atlas & Immerson. He owned a few different operating entities, the largest of which was a private gold and precious metals based investment company.

Sidney Berelson, a certified public accountant with an office on the second floor of our building referred me and our firm to Barry. Sid and I had worked together on a couple of matters over the past years and I found him to be competent and personable. Berelson's firm was engaged to clean up the accounting records and systems in anticipation of the Initial Public Offering of common stock of Vincent's company, Florida Gold Standard Corporation.

Sidney briefed us on Vincent's nagging problems with Florida's regulators. They had made several inquiries concerning the company's solicitation procedures for new investors. Their assertion was that the offers made to new investors represented inadequate disclosures and the ultimate investment represented an alleged sale of securities which were not properly registered. It was an ambiguous area and rather than litigate, a compromise was reached whereby the corporation would file the requisite documents with the Securities and Exchange Commission.

At Berelson's suggestion, I called Vincent to arrange a meeting. He invited Brent and me to his yacht club for lunch. We performed our one-two routine; Brent charmed him and I impressed him. As it turned out, neither was really necessary, he needed a securities firm to guide him through the SEC's public offering process and that was our niche.

Perhaps, with Dad's illness, I took my eye off the ball. Perhaps, the ball was too slippery to keep one's eyes on. Perhaps it was the accountant's responsibility to dissect the ball and understand its true composition. Or, perhaps, as Barry constantly pleaded, the regulators just wanted to take his ball away and close him down. The reality was a combination of all four.

Vincent's enterprises had all of the trappings of success. His offices were well appointed and appropriately staffed. There was an ample research department headed by precious metals mining experts and commodities specialists for complicated futures hedging transactions. Investors were paid regularly with an attractive yield that served well to bring in fresh capital. Gold was king and it appeared that Barry Vincent was my Client from Oz.

Fortunately, I was wise enough to cover all bases recognizing that he just might be the scoundrel that he was accused of being and exercised due diligence, always cognizant of our responsibilities to investors and the rules of my licensing.

I queried the accountants about the quantity and adequacy of the Corporation's gold reserves. They indicated that the inventory was held in safekeeping and that they received written confirmation quantity on-hand from the custodian. The Company's financial viability was predicated on the reserves of precious metals and accordingly, I insisted that Sidney and I visit the vault to "kick the tires" and actually see the bullion.

Vincent's problems mushroomed on multiple fronts as gold stagnated during late 1983 and plummeted during 1984. As it turned out, my suggestion was quite fortuitous to us and the accountants, not so much for Vincent; his actual gold reserves were significantly less than those levels he reported to investors. He was no longer able to attract fresh capital to help him maintain the alleged "Ponzi" based payments he had been paying the Company's investors. Despite his repeated claims that the custodian robbed his metals inventory, the house that Barry built, came tumbling down resulting in yet another Boca Raton financial scandal.

My life was so confused those days. Dad was dying; I was earning huge fees representing a man who was indicted by the state of Florida for fraudulent securities transactions. However, I found the most puzzling thing was that the gold was missing, and I was still not able to conclude whether Vincent was a con man or just conned by one.

Barry sought the services of Lawrence Spencer; a high profile criminal defense attorney to represent him against the charges brought by the state. We continued our engagement in the precarious role of providing background relating to his business practices and securities law to both the prosecution and the defense. To this day, I am not sure which side benefited most from our involvement.

The criminal trial commenced the week that my father died and lasted for five additional weeks. I was not present for jury selection or the respective sides' opening statements. However, I sat beside Spencer through the remainder of the trial, not sure what my actual role was.

The prosecution paraded scores of elderly citizens of our Sunshine State who, after losing their life's savings, would be forced to live their remaining years under the dark non-silver lined clouds purportedly caused by Barry Vincent. The prosecution team engaged experts to convince the jury that Barry's practices of raising new capital amounted to illegal sales of unregistered securities. They concluded with the damning saga of the gold reserves which symbolically, like Old Mother Hubbard's cupboard, were bare.

Their case was persuasive and you could see the emotions steaming in the faces of Barry's family who attended each session sitting in the first row offering him their support. Clearly, it was his son, Dennis, who was the most upset. Was he fearful that the family patriarch would be found guilty and be imprisoned, or was he just an irrational hothead?

Spencer pressed forward with his defense which was primarily hinged on the mysterious disappearance of the safekeeping custodian and, more importantly, the gold. He was traced through Venezuela, and then the trail got cold. Larry strenuously argued that Vincent was duped and, accordingly, how could he be found guilty? In order to counter the state, he presented Defense experts offering testimony of the legality of Vincent's investor solicitation process. Although factual and effective on a professional level, it was tedious for lay people to follow and put the jury to sleep.

It did not, however put Dennis to sleep. He listened to every word and appeared to get more agitated with each progressing facet of Larry's case. When the jury came in with their verdict after a day and a half of deliberation, it was guilty on all counts, Dennis was inconsolable. Predictably, Barry's wife, Paula was visibly upset, his daughter was in tears, but Dennis went on a rampage putting his fist through the sheetrock of the courtroom's wall; ultimately, the Judge instructed the bailiff to remove him from the courtroom.

Barry Vincent was sentenced to twenty five years in an upstate prison. Although the trial provided weeks for them to accept the possibility of a negative verdict, they thought things would work out like always and Barry would be vindicated. Larry Spencer, who was unaccustomed to losing in court attempted to assuage the hurtful feelings of the Vincent family. That was truly an impossible mission given the draconian penalty assessed, especially in the eyes of Dennis who blurted a death wish directed at the defense table implying that all seated there should suffer like his dad.

I remember that day vividly. I had never been that close to a man criminally convicted and sentenced to a long stay in prison. And, although I did not feel responsible for his conviction, I was forced under oath to reveal some very negative things about Barry. As bad as I felt for him, he had a fair trial.

Barry went upstate and his family was forced to adjust to a new normal; one without Mercedes, dining at Boca's best eateries, and having copious amounts of discretionary cash available for frivolity. They had to seek employment, they lost their elegant residence in Boca's Sanctuary, and Paula was forced to file Bankruptcy after the various civil actions depleted any remaining personal funds; shortly thereafter she filed for divorce.

My services were no longer required for either Barry or his family and the remaining Vincent clan scattered like splinters in the wind leaving Boca Raton. So ended the seemingly daily newspaper accounts of the Vincent family and, accordingly, my involvement in their lives.

Six months later, a banner headline in the Palm Beach Post read "Prominent South Florida Attorney Found Dead in Everglades Canal".

Reading on, the article detailed that Lawrence Spencer's vehicle, with him behind the wheel, was found in the water alongside U.S. Highway 27, just north of Boca Raton. Spencer was declared dead at the scene. There were not any witnesses to the event and the tire marks did not suggest anything out of the ordinary.

The story went on to present a litany of his most notorious cases and his accomplishments during his life of sixty-seven years. The presumption was that he was either tired or intoxicated and drove off the roadway. Alcohol and drug screenings were ordered, but were not available at the time of printing. However, toxicology reports later revealed that his blood contained excessive levels of both alcohol and narcotics.

Notwithstanding, the police determined that there was only the slightest hint that foul play had been involved. They went through a perfunctory investigation during the ensuing weeks. Dennis, who I assumed to be behind the travesty, was questioned by the police. His alibi of convenience was that he was shacking up with his girl friend in a motel just outside of Disneyworld. The records reflected that he and she checked into the Orlando flophouse mid-afternoon on that tragic day.

Considering the distance, he would have had ample time to head south to do his work and return to his northern alibi. Was he screwing his girl or screwing the police about his whereabouts when Spencer left the road? She swore that it was the former, and the case hit a dead end.

Larry, with whom I shared many meals, did not drink to excess, but his blood screening reports reflected that his blood alcohol was above legal limits and that there were high levels of Oxycontin in his blood. I knew in my heart that that Dennis was either directly or indirectly involved in this murder. I could not get that image of his eyes shooting darts of hate towards primarily Larry, but also occasionally in my direction as the verdict was read.

Spencer, a defender of the guilty, was never a fan of the authorities and the hastily unfortunate conclusion reached by Palm Beach's finest was that Larry's demise was officially ruled as driving under the influence of drugs resulting in his death.

Larry's death caused me to once again reflect on a separate, but not entirely different, case involving the death of a Miami securities attorney,

Stephen Arky which occurred several years ago. The backdrop of Arky's death was also a financial scandal, but that is where the similarity ended. Arky put a gun in his mouth and said good bye to his problems.

I only knew him by reputation. Arky was about five years older than me in age, but he was light years ahead of me in practice development. He had an unblemished record from his years working at the Securities and Exchange Commission in South Florida, he traveled in the best of circles and had an innate ability to attract new business and solve nasty problems.

His law firm reached full stride during the go-go years in the late 1970's and early 1980's. It had flourished to a two hundred plus staff and it seemed as though they represented every significant publicly owned company in the state.

It was during this time frame that he landed a "cash cow" of a client in the Government Securities business, ESM Securities. Arky befriended the principals, invested his and family members' funds with his client and sat high in his saddle atop Miami's legal circles.

However, there is often darkness at the top of the stairs. In Arky's case, ESM ultimately became the Poster Child of financial scams. The funds they paid out to investors were classically "Ponzi" payments coming from the coffers of newly raised capital.

Their clientele were more sophisticated than Barry Vincent's. They represented major municipalities and the who's who in nationwide banking. When the collapse occurred, more than seventy banks had to close down. This was a scandal of major proportions, even implicating Neil Bush, brother of my soon to be new friends, who was involved in the resulting Savings & Loan Association failures.

Arky spiraled downward into a deep state of depression. He could not face the disgrace that was attendant to this debacle, finding only limited solace with his family and business partners. The emotional pain was so severe that he found his escape in suicide leaving his wife a widow and his children, fatherless.

These two lawyers and their final legal bouts have only the slightest of commonality. However, those threads are intractably woven into the tapestry of my career. My feelings ran the gamut. Naturally I sympathized with their families over their ultimate loss. Both stories serve as reminders that life, both personal and professional, is fragile and events cause turns without warning.

The irony of the sagas of Spencer and Arky is that they are both gone. They are not alive to fight further. Barry Vincent, on the other hand was released after serving eighteen years of his sentence. Two years have elapsed since his parole and I have not heard from him. I have, however, been informed of Vincent sightings around town. I am not surprised that he has not contacted me. I would guess that he expected a stronger effort from me in his defense. Such was certainly the case with his son, Dennis. Apparently, and quite fortunately in my opinion, he held me less responsible for its outcome than he did Larry Spencer.

Unfortunately, we cannot erase time without dealing with the consequences of events occurring long past.

CHAPTER 9

WEDNESDAY AFTERNOON - EVENING

Once again, the mood changer Rachel alerted me, "David, there is an Ethan Gold on the phone. He says that it's personal."

I probed my memory, but could not come up with a match. I pondered, who in the hell he was, when the thought came that it might be the Ethan that my daughter, Darlene was dating. "Hello, this is David Atlas, how can I help you" was my perfunctory opening.

"Hello sir…Mr. Atlas. I hope that you remember me because… uhm….I was hoping to do this in person…..I love Darlene and more than anything I want to marry her. I intend to ask her tonight at dinner. I sure hope it is OK with you and Mrs. Atlas. Uhm."

Was this guy for real? Get a pair of balls mister. "Wow, this is kind of sudden" I interjected giving him a second to gather himself and collect his thoughts, although he probably would need a month. "My wife mentioned just yesterday that you guys are coming in next weekend and that you are trying to arrange a dinner with us and your parents."

"I spoke with my mom and dad, and they are quite excited."

They should be excited. Ethan is a lucky guy; Darlene is quite a prize. Far be it for me to spoil their excitement, I continued our dialogue with, "Mrs. A and I look forward to meeting them." Mrs. A and I also look forward to knowing him a little better. After all, I was not sure I could pick him out of a line-up. Despite wanting to offer up a sarcastic remark, I fought it off and said "I can not wait for Darlene's phone call this evening when you present the dessert to her." Of course, meaning the ring and not his version of dessert.

"Does that mean it is okay with you?" he asked as though he was a kid who wanted another piece of candy. He was and he did.

"If Darlene loves you as much as you apparently do her, you have our blessings." It then occurred to me that perhaps I should have discussed this with Elaine first. However, it really did not make much difference: Darlene was going to do what Darlene wanted to do. In all matters including love and war, she has a mind of her own.

I had already determined that Elaine was home and a quick glance at my watch informed me that it was 4:45 PM I decided to fold Wednesday's tent and call it a day. And, what a day it had been. I dialed the house and on the second ring she answered. "Hi babe", I greeted. "If you haven't started dinner yet, why don't you meet me at Houston's for drinks and something to eat?"

"What's going on?" she asked inquisitively, yet intuitively knowing something was out of the norm.

"Well, we have a lot to talk about. There is the SEC and Washington about which you didn't sound too enthusiastic earlier. And, more importantly, a new unrelated wrinkle just developed in the last ten minutes. The Jerk, Ethan, just called and asked permission for Darlene's hand in matrimony."

"Stop calling him a Jerk, he is-going to be our son-in-law."

Well, so much for my not having discussed the matter with her prior to offering Ethan our approval. "He's going to ask her tonight after their dinner date and I suspect that Darlene will call us immediately thereafter. So, let's meet at the Big H for an early dinner. I will meet you there in forty minutes. I love you."

"What a week, first the cruise and now a wedding to plan" she responds as enthusiastically as Ethan, however considerably more focused, and as an after-thought, she added, "Oh, I love you too."

Oh, Thanks!

Nothing like a wedding to deplete the bank account and help obviate any concerns she might have had about shuttling between South Florida and D.C. Who knows maybe W would come to the wedding. I made a note that if she decided to invite Randall Savage, I y111r

would make an investment in Grey Goose's parent corporation prior to the big day.

Into the intercom, "Rachel, I'm calling it quits for the day. See you tomorrow."

Out of the intercom, "So, who is this Ethan Silver?"

Perhaps, for the last time I replied, "A Jerk."

The ride to Houston's was uneventful and notwithstanding my journey of twenty five miles compared to Elaine's four, I arrived before her and could have finished *War and Peace* before her appearance. I snatched two seats at the bar knowing that the regulars would be marching in shortly and ordered my celebratory cocktail, Kettle One on the rocks. Aptly, my usual philosophy prevailed; my glass was half filled, when I saw her pull into the parking lot. I drained the remaining fluid, requested another and a glass of white zinfandel for Elaine.

Kiss kiss hug hug, as she questioned, "Can you believe that our Darlene is getting married?"

"A toast to My Little Girl and …Ethan," I offered, careful not to call him that J word.

Considering that she had only of forty minutes to get dressed and, I might add, did so wonderfully, as well as to call the immediate world, it was amazing that she also composed the written outline of wedding details she had to handle.

I served up my usual dose of logic, "Don't you think that we should wait until we hear from Darlene before you call the caterer and hire a band?"

She served up hers, "Men are such Jerks. I was speaking to her when Ethan called you. She will act surprised, but she has been expecting this for several weeks. She even saw her ring last night, when he left the room to get a beer." Why was I always the last to hear about these things?

More importantly, did she have to remind me that Darlene spent so much time in Ethan's room? And, why do I have to refrain from using the word Jerk word when she can use it at will? Jewish wives can say whatever they want, a privilege not extended to their husbands; yet, another entry to be made in my *Ode to the Jewish Husband*. My only logical response was, "Another Kettle One on the rocks please." However, I decided to call it quits with that drink as I wanted to be able to speak to Darlene when she called and did not want to sound too much like her soon to be uncle, Randall Savage.

I settled the tab with the barmaid and escorted Elaine to the hostess who in turn showed us to our table.

"Lenny and Michael are so excited. They are getting another brother," was her opening gambit of table talk.

How did they know him and to me he was only a casual acquaintance? Once again, "Don't you think you should wait until it is official?"

"It's official; I even spoke with Ethan's mother."

I needed to change the subject; I was not winning that debate. I would just put a hundred grand into the bank and hand over the checkbook. "Speaking of done deals, have you given any further consideration to the SEC matter?"

"David, if it happens, I will be right by your side. The remainder of the term for your appointment would be only two and a half years, and during most of that time I'll be busy planning the wedding. I'm really excited."

What's the If? And. which of the two was she really excited about? Oh well, it did not matter.

The remaining dinner conversation was divided appropriately between the two topics: 99% on the wedding, 1% on Washington, D.C. After coffee, I walked Elaine to her car, gave her a quick peck on the cheek as she removed her cell phone from her purse; once again demonstrating her priorities in life.

It took me five minutes to get home; it took Elaine two phone calls. We were together in the family room when *THE* phone call came. I do not know why, but Elaine allowed me to answer the phone. "Hi daddy" was the same greeting that I have received since her Kindergarten days; enough to melt ice. In fact, I thought back to my young daughter in those innocent days. Where has the time gone?

"Hi sweetheart, how are you?" my designated phone greeting to her.

"I'm getting married!"

"I know; I spoke with Ethan earlier today." His act of actually asking my permission was a good indication of his upbringing. Difficult as it was, he earned some points in my book. "You guys must really be excited. Mom and I are. She has already called the immediate world, so I am glad that you said yes when he proposed."

"I can't wait for you and mom to see the ring. We are coming home next week-end and you will get a chance to meet his folks. Let me speak to mom." I guess she had enough of the Old Man.

"Before I put her on, put Ethan on, I want to congratulate him." She put the Jerk on, "Hi, Ethan, congratulations and welcome to the family. You be sure you take care of my little girl."

"I will, she's my girl now," he replied.

Careful Jerk, she is still my girl. "Hold on Mrs. A…er… mom, wants to say hello."

Elaine had a short sentence or two with Ethan and he turned the phone over to Darlene who managed to engage in a two hour marathon with Elaine; no doubt a women thing. He had better get used to it. I was already watching the evening news when Elaine apparently ran out of breath and had to get off the phone. The lead story was a feature showing Jeb Bush visiting his brother in the White House.

I did not pay much attention to the babble about the unofficial family visit with the brothers and their parents. I was reflecting on my luncheon earlier and anticipated that Jeb was working his magic behind the scenes on Carlos' behalf with me as the ultimate beneficiary.

Elaine made her appearance in our bedroom as the evening sports spot which was focused on the Dolphins preparation for Saturday's opening day was winding down. I was also winding down and ready to spend the next seven hours with Mr. Sandman. She on the other hand, got her second wind and wanted to gab about the wedding. "Honey, we will have plenty of time for that, I need to get some sleep……..unless you want to…."

She cut me off, "You are truly a Jerk. We will also have plenty of time for that."

I surrendered, "Good night, Doll. " Four nanoseconds later I was fast asleep.

CHAPTER 10

THURSDAY MORNING

The sun was bright; the sky was the purest of blues with nary a cloud in sight, all the indications of a grand day. I pulled into the garage, took my designated spot and was feeling so good that I would have taken the steps rather than the elevator were it not for the seventeen flights between the lower level and the office. Instead, I opted for the Otis Express.

I was in the cheeriest of moods, "Good morning Janice, good morning Ed, good morning Cathy….." all before I reached Rachel's unattended desk. I was so happy that I did not mind getting my own coffee. Not that it mattered; I would have had to retrieve it myself anyway.

As it was only 7:45 AM, I had to expect it was too early to receive the phone call from Savage. I logged on to my computer and opened the work-in progress files to determine if there was any invoicing to be done prior to my departure on Friday. Billing was one of my favorite pastimes in the office, trumped only by cash collections.

The instruction sheet to the Accounting Department was straightforward; progress bill Mid-Florida Cattle Consortium $35,000, final bill SSI Securities $375,000 and make sure that Brent is given a list of all his past-due accounts for follow-up before I return to the office on Tuesday.

It was 8:30 AM and could Rachel have arrived and been at her desk? Seeking the answer, I probed, "Rachel, are you there?"

My question was answered with the predictable pre-9:00 AM response: Silence. My giddy anticipatory mood was still prevailing, so I left my post to pour my second cup of caffeine for the morning. The water-cooler chatter in the coffee room was focused on the Dolphin-Titan contest two days off. Not interested, I made an early retreat to my office.

En route, I passed Brent's workday habitat and sometimes evening playground. I noticed that he was on the phone and could not avoid overhearing him say, "Yes, Dennis, one hundred percent he'll be there tomorrow by 3:00 – 3:30 in the afternoon. Yes, I'll see you this afternoon as planned."

Anticipating the call from Savage, Jeb or, even, the White House, I paid little attention to my partner's conversation, but it did register enough to leave a mark in my mind that nagged me over the coming days. I later realized that I should have questioned him about it on the spot. Hindsight is always twenty-twenty!

Back in my office, "Rachel, are you there?"

At her desk, but not yet having put away her purse or settling in for the day, she replied, "Of course I am. I've been here for about a half hour."

Why did I and do I put up with this nonsense? "Did I receive any calls while I was getting my own coffee?"

"No, why didn't you ask me to get it for you?"

It is no wonder that she often left me feeling as though I were traveling through the Twilight Zone.

Speaking of the Twilight Zone, within seconds of finishing with Rachel, Judith's voice buzzed through the intercom speakers. "David, have you got a few minutes to meet with Deborah and me to go over a few things on the prospectus?"

Without hesitation, "No, I've got too much going on before I leave tomorrow. You've been through dozens of these things, I'm sure you can handle it." Thinking of my last encounter with that duo, the last thing I needed that morning was to be with them when the big call came in.

She respectfully indicated, "Okay, I'll have a draft of the document for your review before you leave today and you can read it on the plane tomorrow."

I suspect that it would have been a pleasurable meeting, but sometimes one has to think beyond instant gratification, "Thank you. I'll see you later."

I certainly had a busy morning waiting for the call. I finished my first Sudoku and was contemplating starting another or playing a mind numbing game of solitaire on the computer. Figuring that I would be seeing enough cards over the weekend, I turned the page opting for a second number's puzzle. Before I could fill in two boxes, the anticipated call arrived.

"David, Russell Savage is on line three."

"Hi, Russell, I've been expecting your call." I was really hoping that it would be the White House or Jeb who called, but beggars can not be choosers. If he had delivered the news in person, a glass of vodka would have already been poured, but since he was on the phone, I guess that he was drinking from his own stock.

"Davey boy, we're in," was his greeting line. Davey Boy; where in the hell did he get that one? And, what was with the, *we*?

"Great, fill in the missing pieces," I responded trying to sound professional, busy and pleased simultaneously.

He filled me in, "Sorry that I didn't get back to you yesterday, but it was late when the governor called. The president agreed with his brother and he will be making the announcement either Thursday or Friday of next week. He would like to meet with you at the White House on Thursday; his staff will contact you about the timing including an invitation for you and your wife to a dinner to be held on Friday evening honoring our new ambassador to Vietnam."

Wow, talk about life in the fast lane! I would get home from Vegas on Tuesday morning and Elaine and I would be off to Washington on Wednesday; Thursday and Friday would be with W and a bunch of other big shots and the week-end to find a part-time residence.

Savage went on to tell me that he would like to meet with me prior to my West Wing audience and that he was not invited. He suggested that we book rooms at the Hayes-Adams Hotel (I would not have had it any other way) and meet on Wednesday afternoon for cocktails (he would not have had it any other way).

Without divulging too much information, I shared with Russell that I would be out of town for the week-end, but back in the office on Tuesday. I assured him that I would make the room reservations and that Elaine and I would meet him on Wednesday around 6:00 PM We exchanged cellular phone numbers and I informed him that I would let him know if any changes were required once I heard from Washington.

I went on-line and learned that the recently appointed Ambassador to the Socialist Republic of Vietnam was Michael W. Marine and called Rachel, "R, have Deborah add to the file she's preparing for me on the SEC, I also need background information on Michael W. Marine."

"What's going on?" she queried.

"Get Deborah going on this; I'll need it for my plane ride, and then come in here" was my response as I dialed Elaine's cell phone. I knew she would not be home; I was correct she was already checking out the bridal salons on Worth Avenue.

"Hi, Sweetheart, while you're out shopping, pick up a fancy dress; we're going to a formal dinner at the White House next Friday."

"What are you talking about?" she asked incredulously "We're meeting Darlene's future in-laws on Saturday."

"Savage just called and though I've not heard from the White House yet, he assures me that I will soon and we'll be Washington bound next Wednesday for a Thursday one-on-one with the president and then a dinner dance on Friday. Not bad for two kids from Brooklyn! Call Darlene and push things back a week; we won't be home from D.C. in time for Ethan's parents."

"I'm sure that they'll understand. David, should I cancel my week-end; shouldn't you cancel yours?" was Elaine's way too logical response.

Rachel broke in on the intercom, "David, what the hell is going on? The White House Office of the Chief of Staff is on the phone; line four."

"Babe, I'll get back to you, the White House is on the phone."

"Knock 'em dead, Sweetheart. See you later."

I was greeted on the phone by Andy Card's secretary who informed me in rapid order that a meeting would be held in the West Wing on Thursday with the president, Mr. Card and William Donaldson, Chairman of the Securities and Exchange Commission at 2:00 PM In addition, Elaine and I would be guests at the formal dinner in the East Room on Friday evening. She requested either Elaine's number or Rachel's in order for the administration's Social Secretary to call with all the missing logistical pieces.

I quickly found out how an efficient office operates. That momentous call lasted less than one minute and was ultimately the catalyst to a chain reaction of changes in my personal and professional life.

Within three seconds of hanging up, Rachel burst into my office, "David, the whole staff is buzzing about the call from the White House. What's going on?"

"It appears that the rumors are not rumors. I'm meeting with the President and Chairman of the SEC next week to discuss my filling the vacant seat on the Commission."

I went on to tell her that the Washington responsibilities would not be full time; that I would be commuting between Palm Beach and D.C. on a regular basis and that an acting managing partner would have to be named to take over my day-to-day responsibilities at AI&S. Further, I informed her that the partners were just as aware of the rumors as I was and that I did not to want make any formal firm announcement until I returned from Washington.

"How does Elaine feel about this?" Couldn't she come up with a more pertinent question?

"She's excited, but much more so with the wedding plans."

"What wedding plans?"

"Darlene is getting married to that guy, Ethan, who called me yesterday afternoon."

"Why am I always the last one to find out about things?"

"No, I am. Can you get me a cup of coffee?" I asked.

"No, I have to call Elaine. Get it yourself, Mr. Commissioner."

So much for not making any formal announcement to the staff; within minutes, I was receiving congratulatory phone calls from all my partners, except Brent, and most of the senior level associates. What in the hell was going on with Brent? I would have to get that matter resolved after I returned on Tuesday.

Yes, notwithstanding all else going on in my life, I had decided to still go on my mini-vacation to Las Vegas.

Discretion is the better part of valor; Rachel walked into my office with a mug of coffee and the usual back-up supply in a carafe. I sipped the brew as I pictured the limousine dropping Elaine and me off under the portico to the White House.

Darlene would have a spectacular wedding, but it would not meet the splendor of a routine Friday night dinner dance with the president and other dignitaries. The cuisine would be gourmet at both, but the culinary skills of the White House chefs would certainly overshadow Palm Beach's finest. This was going to be my life for the next two years.

My mind drifted off; the East Room was elegant and the band was wonderful. Thankfully, they were playing a waltz; one to which I could dance. Elaine and I were gliding over the dance floor making moves I never knew I had. I feel a tap on my shoulder turning to see the president cutting in requesting to dance with my bride; leaving his as my new partner. As the dance tune ended, W and I gave our partners a little love tap on their respective behinds. Perhaps I really am a Republican!

Usually it would be Rachel, but this time it was Ed Sheerson's voice that came out of the intercom interrupting the scene, "David, how about Epstein's for lunch?"

"Meet ya at the elevator in five minutes."

I guess it would now be obligatory that the President and First Lady be invited to our gala, and stranger things have happened, they might actually come. That would give the new in-laws something to talk about.

Peering up at Dad's portrait, "What do you think about your son now?"

Although I knew it was impossible, his smile appeared a bit wider and his shoulders more upright.

CHAPTER 11

THURSDAY AFTERNOON

It was still sunny, high seventies and low humidity; a beautiful south Florida day, so we decided to traverse the three blocks to Epstein's by foot. The short outbound hike provided an excellent opportunity to update Ed on the events of the last few days relative to the SEC and there was little doubt that the lunch to be consumed would be digested better with the walk back to the office.

By the time that I completed substantially the same Securities and Exchange briefing provided to Rachel just minutes earlier, we had arrived at the deli and ordered our lunch. While munching on my sandwich and washing it down with a Dr. Brown's Diet Black Cherry soda, I added, "Assuming all goes as expected, I will have to step down temporarily from my day-to-day responsibilities and I would like you to be our acting managing partner during my stint in Washington."

Ed was genuinely surprised and said, "Thanks Dave, I'm flattered but, you must know that this is going to hit Brent hard. He's more senior than me and he's already pissed off about your faux pas at the dinner party last week at Peter's house."

"What are you talking about?"

"Perhaps, I shouldn't have said anything, but Jennifer found out about his affair and he thinks that she overheard your comments to him at the party. You were apparently chiding him when she returned from the restroom."

"Well, that explains his chillier than normal attitude of recent days, but you know that I'm more discrete than that. I immediately changed the topic when she approached us. I'll have to clear the air when we get back to the office."

The remainder of the lunch was routine; the usual dose of small talk. We shared updates on the kids; his daughter, Doreen was in her senior year at George Washington University in D.C., I'd have to look her up; and his son, Nathan was progressing nicely towards his MBA at Florida. The conversation provided the perfect segue to the Atlas' current event; Darlene's wedding. We were metaphorically patting each other's backs as we declined dessert and asked our server for the check.

The banter during our return trip to the office was not as spirited as was the first leg. My mind was preparing for the bout with Brent to resolve the nonsense of my culpability with respect to his marital problems. Although my office takes up the south corner, upon arriving at the reception desk, I turned north for Brent's office.

He was not at his desk so I went to Janice, his secretary "When will Brent be back?"

She explained that he left just after 1:00 PM and, "He told me that he had an out of office meeting and would not be back until tomorrow morning."

"Who is he meeting with?" I probed.

"That's the strange thing. He always tells me, but not this time. He was vague and said I should only call his mobile phone if it was an emergency."

It was strange indeed. All partners were generally familiar with our peers' schedules and this was not mentioned at the partners' luncheon on Tuesday. I assumed he was with his paramour, but perhaps it was something else.

I obviously had too many things on my mind as the Brent matter had worked its way down my priority list by the time I reached Rachel's desk. Hardly believing my eyes: she was there. "Any calls while I was gone?"

She quickly responded, "Just your son, Michael. He says everything is good, he just wanted to speak with you before you head west and that he would be on a date tonight and in class tomorrow; give him a call on his cell if you have the chance."

Michael is our youngest son and was in his second year at the University of South Florida. Because of the six year gap between him and Lenny, he was home alone while his siblings were off to college. It was during that period that he and I developed our special bond that flourishes through the present day.

We always discussed my gaming ventures and he became so enthralled with casinos that his eighteenth birthday present was a jaunt to the Bahamas with his brother, Lenny and me providing his initiation into the real world casinos. Unfortunately, he won; there was no turning back. Next year, when he turns twenty-one, the three musketeers will go out to Vegas in order to celebrate; we may even invite my upcoming son-in-law, Ethan. I guess I created a Frankenstein.

It was a toss-up as to whether he wanted to discuss my upcoming outing or Darlene's upcoming nuptials. Considering the closeness of our family, the only real toss-up was which would come first.

After one ring and his phone's apparent caller ID option, Michael answered, "Hi Pops, how about that Darlene?" Mystery solved.

"Yeah! Hi, Mikie, how are you?"

"Things are cool here in Tampa, but it sounds like there's a lot going on in your life. Mom filled me in with the Washington news, but we both know it's tomorrow that you're really thinking about."

"That's my boy! By this time tomorrow I should be over Tampa heading west. Look out your window."

"I'll bet you're staying at the Paris Hotel. Is that cute dealer, Yvette still there?"

"You win and I'll let you know. Plan on coming home the week-end after next. We're going to meet Ethan's family."

"OK, dad. Have a great time in Vegas and we'll talk after you get home."

"Love ya, Mikie."

Click!

Looking up to the portrait, "Yeah Dad, he's got the problem. He'll tell Elaine he loves her, but I only get it on birthday cards. Not to worry, we'll get to him sooner than you and I did."

I noticed that either Rachel or Deborah placed two files in my in-box: The SEC - its organization, résumé's of Chairman and Commissioners, Recent Rulings, and Current Staff Proposals; Michael W. Marine – Background Research and Summary of U.S. Relations with the Socialist Republic of Vietnam

I picked up the Ambassador's folder and started reading about his recent appointment by President Bush. He would be leaving for Vietnam just after the dinner in his honor next Friday evening. Although he would be arriving in Ho Chi Minh City, F.K.A. Saigon this month, it was almost thirty years ago that I was leaving for Southeast Asia; another lifetime ago.

I recalled arriving at the Oakland Army Base at the designated day and hour and was greeted in the same friendly manner as experienced at the Draft Board: Go sign in and wait for instructions. The base served as the transition facility for all troops going to stations in the Pacific. Upon signing in, I noticed a bulletin board above the sign-in desk with the posting: Personnel with The Following MOS (Military Occupation Specialty) Report to Desk Two. The list contained seven jobs, of which mine, Clerk Typist was the second. At Desk Two, I learned that there were too many with my MOS in Vietnam and that those coming through that day were going to have their orders changed to Hawaii.

After signing in Desk One, the troops went for Jungle Fatigues, Jungle Shots, and Jungle Prayers and then waited for the next plane to Hell. After signing in at Desk Two, the troops went and got lei-ed, except for me of course, I immediately called Elaine and told her to practice the hula.

Formations were convened three times a day alerting the assembled masses of the passenger manifest for the upcoming flights. At the noon briefing the Sergeant yelled: The following personnel are leaving for Okinawa – five names. The following personnel are leaving for Guam – three names. The following personnel are leaving for Honolulu – ten names, mine not included. And finally, the following personnel are leaving for Vietnam's transition point, Long Bihn – two hundred names.

Such was the routine three times daily until my third day. At the morning formation, the names of the few elite non-war zone candidates were read and then came the Vietnam brigade. Sure enough, my name was the first called. I rushed up to the podium and proudly stated "Sergeant, I'm going to Hawaii; they're changing my orders; there are too many clerks in Vietnam."

In true military fashion, "Are you Atlas, 135-74-3176?"

"But Sarge, you don't understand, they said they're changing my orders."

"Are you Atlas, 135-74-3176? You'd better rush and get your shots and jungle issue boy. The plane is leaving in two hours."

You can't fight City Hall, and you can't modify the Army way. Our encounter was a little longer than the two step verbal exchange presented, but the end result was the same. I had two hours to ready myself for the flight to Vietnam; more importantly, I was forewarned that there were already too many Remington Raiders in 'Nam and fully understood that every soldier's secondary specialty was that of Infantry Rifleman.

More importantly, my allotted time did not provide the opportunity to call Elaine. She was euphoric about our pending move to Honolulu. We did ultimately get there on a Rest and Recuperation (R&R) visit six months later, but she had no idea that at that moment, I was on my way to Southeast Asia.

We flew east on a civilian flight complete with movies and meals. However, all signs of civility were gone as we approached Bien Hoa, the airport facility supporting Long Bihn. The flight attendant announced, "In the unlikely event of an attack, there would be bunkers to the front and rear of the plane." Prior to such warning, I was naively lulled into thinking that all I had to worry about was buckling my seat belt and knowing where to locate the floatation device.

The new and stark reality came upon exiting the plane and melting in the 120 degree sauna that was to be my home for the next year.

It was a quick truck ride to a huge compound where substantially the same formation and assignment drill of Oakland was performed, in reverse three times daily. In this instance, we were waiting to be assigned to a unit and until one's number was pulled out of the box, he had the privilege of pulling Kitchen duty, filling sand bags, incinerating latrine waste or whatever other menial task the Army regulars could dream up.

Being a Brooklyn Boy, I searched for the Quonset hut with wires coming in, presuming it to be the place where orders arrived, and volunteered my services as a runner or whatever else they needed. It must have been Divine Intervention. The Duty Officer was Joshua Cohen from Cincinnati. Thinking that we must have been the only two Jews in Vietnam, I symbolically recited my Bar Mitzvah speech to alert him that we were Hebraic brothers; as it turned out, we did both belong to the same college fraternity, Alpha Epsilon Pi.

My assessment of the function performed at Josh's office was correct and he made my three days there tolerable, repeatedly assuring me that he would get me a prime assignment. True to his word, I watched the incoming teletype assigning Atlas, David 135-74-3176, to a Headquarters unit in Saigon as a Clerk Typist.

Within a month of arriving in country, the eight other clerks in my unit were rotated home leaving me the most senior clerk in the Security, Plans and Operations Unit. I picked up the Colonel at his hotel each morning, dropped him off after work and had access to his jeep at all other times. There could not have been more than ten better jobs for a draftee in Vietnam. Thanks, Josh!

My home was a small compound of about 150 non-commissioned personnel located between the Third Field Hospital and Tan Son Nhut Air Base. It appeared relatively secure, but was overrun by the enemy during the Tet Offensive several years prior to my service. Pictures of the massacre were posted on the walls to obviate any sense of complacency; after all, we were in a Combat Zone and it could happen again at any time.

During those Army days, I would pass the United State Embassy everyday. Years later the war was over and we lost. President Clinton normalized relations with the North Vietnamese victor a decade ago; and next week I would be one of the White House's invited guests honoring our new Ambassador to Vietnam. It is interesting how some threads weave their way through one's life tapestry; Vietnam is certainly a prominent thread in mine.

CHAPTER 12

THURSDAY EVENING

I did not want to start a new trend. Thursday would have been the third consecutive day that I left early. However, this was an exceptional week and under the circumstances, I would have just been spinning wheels watching the clock if I did not leave.

I cleared my desk, searching one more time for something that needed my immediate attention. I decided that the only thing requiring my immediate attention was the ignition switch of my car.

"Rachel!" Miracles of miracles, she was at her desk.

"Yes, Mr. Commissioner," she responded finally with a modicum of respect, but not completely void of sarcasm. No difference, I liked how it sounded.

"There's not much that I need to do around here and I've got tons of things to go over with Elaine before we leave, so I'm getting out early. See ya when I get back from Vegas. Thanks for your help during the last day or two."

"Have a great time, David. I'll hold down the fort tomorrow and Monday." Her gesture, of course meant that she would arrive around 9:30 each morning, take an extended lunch, and beat the traffic home by leaving at 4:30 PM

I stopped at my door turning to take one last visual inventory of the office, switched the lights off, and I mentally shifted gears into neutral hanging up a *Gone Fishin* sign. I was a free man until Tuesday!

The drive home was completely uneventful; my thoughts were a mosaic of Vegas, Washington, Brent Immerson and the wedding, each one having almost equal representation. Although I was excited about going, the other matters were certainly significant and managed to ebb my usual unbridled joy about going to David's Disneyworld.

I parked my Benz in the garage and entered the house through the laundry room, by the dinning room and, reminiscent of Tuesday evening, still did not find Elaine. She was sitting at her desk in the kitchen in full battle mode; phone on her shoulder, pen in hand making entries on her wedding list, and the latest copy of Modern Bride opened halfway through. I guessed that she had not heard from the White House or clearly she should have had a different set of priorities.

Considerately, she ended the call quickly whereupon I gave her a kiss on the cheek and a squeeze of her behind. "Hi babe, you didn't hear from the White House?"

Handing me a notepad, she said "Yeah, I wrote down all the details; here's the list." Once again, she sounded less than enthusiastic, but she added "I can't believe we're going to a Presidential Dinner."

"Me neither, things are really moving fast. We have a lot of balls up in the air."

I read through the protocol as she dialed Darlene's cell phone. It appeared that my daughter's selection of certain flowers was obviously more important than what Laura would be wearing next Friday. After reading through her detailed notes, I more fully understood the who's, the how's, the where's and the when's of a meeting with the President and attendance at one of his social functions. She was still talking with Darlene, so I re-read the notes in order to avoid committing a professional or social breach of etiquette.

Still gabbing away, I could have repeated the process five or six times and she would still be on the phone. Instead, I decided to commence dinner preparation. Elaine had already set aside the fish and vegetables intended for our evening repast in the refrigerator. The mahi-mahi was marinating in a citrus blend and the broccoli and carrots were washed and waiting to be placed in a steaming colander.

I set the table, started water for the vegetables and fired up the grill on the patio to the requisite pre-heat setting. Poised for action, I was circling the ranch waiting for clearance to land; her hanging up the phone. She noticed my culinary progress and again, considerately, ended the call quickly. That is to say if an hour and twenty minutes is quickly.

I opened a bottle of Chardonnay and we toasted each other for the triad of our good fortune for the week: Darlene's wedding, the presidential appointment and, last but not least, my Vegas and her Caribbean cruise. A short kiss and I was off to the patio; she was off to the stove.

Grilled and steamed, our respective dishes were completed and plated simultaneously. We enjoyed the quiet of our dinner on the patio. The wine, lake and gorgeous Florida sunset blended together, to create a magical experience.

Elaine says, "David, I am excited about Washington and I'll be with you every step of the way…" BUT? "Washington is primarily for you; Darlene's wedding is for us."

Another chapter in the *Ode to the Jewish Husband*; she is always right!

The dichotomy of these events would present challenges, but we each recognized that I would rely on her to make Darlene's big day as wonderful as possible; and she relied on me to progress further professionally for the betterment of us and the kids.

It was amazing how we both came to the same conclusion through the calm words and body language of the other. That being resolved, we were able to start packing, putting the first two priorities on the back burner until next week.

She more than I, but we were both giddy about our respective getaways. I have enjoyed comparable outings several times a year, but Elaine had never been away either solo or with just a friend. It was the most opportune time; I had my agenda and she had hers, and I suspected that she and Susan would be "weddinged" out by the time they got home. Me, on the other hand, would doubtlessly have tales of spectacular gaming sessions and would be accompanied home with an armored vehicle.

After our individual packing efforts of twenty minutes and two hours, respectively, the result was one bag for me and three pieces of luggage for her. Same duration away; and yet, she requires three times as much baggage. That was normal; however, it was quite unusual that they would be checked in for differing destinations.

I was already done with the evening bathroom drill and watching the news when Elaine came in. I had already decided that I did not want to be called a Jerk again, so I leaned over and kissed her goodnight.

As I have said before, I am always the last to know what is going on. Such was the case that evening. Before my head hit the pillow, Elaine was all over me like a cat in heat. Not the laundry room, but a great surprise none the less and a grand way to start our vacations.

I was truly blessed with a wonderful life and as an added feature; I would be leaving Dodge tomorrow.

CHAPTER 13

FRIDAY MORNING

"Get up….get outa bed…..drag a comb across your head," was the Beatles' morning message and often the mantra I mouthed while readying myself in the AM. Especially, that morning; it was our time to escape the demands of the past week, relax and upon our respective returns, prepare for the one upcoming highlighted by meeting the President and First Lady.

Within hours, Thelma and Louise would be off to the Caribbean and me to the neon wonderland in Nevada.

Predictably, I was the first one in the kitchen. The coffee maker was switched on, my bagel was placed in our new toaster oven and I went out to get the morning paper. I was able to take my leave, as the new appliance came with the guarantee that I no longer needed to be there to catch my toasted treats, which theretofore were launched from the toaster in an exact trajectory to the sink's disposal unit.

It was a wonderful September morning; sunny, mid-seventies and a cloudless azure Florida sky. I was reading the paper on the patio and enjoying my breakfast as I watched the dozens of ducks and occasional egret and blue herons that accent the lake. After a half hour, Elaine joined me holding a cup of coffee.

"What a gorgeous day," she said.

"What a gorgeous woman," I replied.

"Nice try, Romeo. What time do we need to leave? I still have a few things that I have to get done."

"We should leave here around ten o'clock. That way you'll be at Susan's with about twenty minutes to spare before your limo gets there. You've got about an hour."

I poured my second cup and focused on a family of ducks paddling across the lake. They reached the far shore just as I finished my java, I wished them a good day, a good week-end, for that matter, and headed inside to get dressed, load the bags in the car, and wait for Elaine.

At five minutes before ten, I was in the car in the driveway ready to beep the horn to get her attention, when out came Elaine. Perhaps we had another entry into *Ode to the Jewish Husband*; when it is something the husband wants, she will always be late, when it is the other way around, you can invariably expect timeliness. Adhering to such maxim, this was her adventure also and she was floating down the driveway eager to get an early start to her day.

I navigated out of the neighborhood and onto Glades Road heading west to Susan's place. She lives on the periphery of the Everglades just about the westernmost development within Boca Raton. As the bird flies, less than a mile from where Larry Spencer's body was found years ago. Why would that memory pop into my mind today?

It would be fifteen minutes before we reached the interim destination; from there I would get on the turnpike northbound heading for Palm Beach International Airport.

It might have been her three cups of coffee; it might have been the anticipation of finally getting away on a girlie week-end; or most probably equal parts of each, but Elaine became an absolute chatterbox once we were driving. And, surprisingly, her thoughts were all vacation oriented, not those of the wedding.

Since they were only taking a four day cruise, the itinerary was limited to one day on Carnival Cruise Lines' private island and one day in Nassau, she intended to baste like a turkey on their beach and by the pool on sea days, and shop for a ring and necklace in the Bahamas on their day in port.

Her mouth was moving at a hundred miles an hour. I was only willing to commit ten percent of my concentration to her incessant babble. My occasional "that's nice" apparently was all she needed to not feel completely alone in the car. I had much more important matters to focus on. And, surprisingly, my thoughts were all vacation oriented, not those of Washington.

Time flies when you are having a good time. Such was the case that Friday morning. Before we realized it, we were in Susan's driveway. Elaine flew out the car to her friend's open arms, her mouth still in high gear not skipping a word. I removed her bags from the trunk and left them in front of the garage door awaiting their limousine ride to the cruise terminal.

I gave each of the ladies a peck on the cheek and offered my wishes for a bon voyage and returned to my car for the half hour drive to the airport. Buckled in the Benz, I opened my window and blew Elaine another kiss, and shouted "I love you. Have a great time. I'll see you on Tuesday."

I think she heard me. She was still talking full speed ahead, but by then her monologue became a conversation, as Susan was also gabbing away uncontrollably; the dueling banjos of their chatter created a volley of words not humanly fathomable except to them. Such was the official start of their four day talkathon and my private retreat to Las Vegas.

The last leg of my morning drive was taking the turnpike north to Southern Boulevard and then east into Palm Beach International Airport. PBI is not a world class airport, the international in its name results from occasional flights into or from the Caribbean. It is however, a very pleasant facility with beautifully landscaped interiors and exteriors providing a tastefully appointed tropical ambience combined with an efficient delivery of their primary mission; air travel.

The new normal resulting from post September 11 security demands required arrival at the airport about an hour and a half prior to flight time on travel days. For my Vegas journey I had an extra cushion. After finding a good spot in the long-term lot and checking my bag, it was just after 11:00 AM and my scheduled departure was 1:00 PM

I scanned the Departures Board to see if there were any updates. Predictably, it indicated that Delta Flight 711 would be delayed an estimated hour. Wonderful!

First Doc crapped out, to put it in the gaming vernacular, and then came the news that the flight would be delayed. Why is it that most things never go as planned? Nonsense, in the larger picture, these were only minor inconveniences; in a few hours I would be in Las Vegas.

Sam Snead's Lounge is located in the center of the airport and is a wonderful venue for idling away time until departure. There are photographs and paraphernalia of historical golfing events and the lounge's namesake is prominent in the décor. The menu is ample and the food is better than expected, the selection of wines and spirits is extensive, and adjoining the pub is a large putting green available for practice while waiting or keeping one's children occupied while the parent is otherwise occupied.

I selected a table overlooking the faux grass putting surface and offering a panoramic window vista of the two concourses' arrivals and departures, including my intended gate. The Departures Board had not been changed; the scheduled departure was still reading 2:00 PM It was not even noon; and I still had hours to go. However, as Jimmy Buffet suggests, *It's Five O'clock Somewhere*, I ordered my first potent beverage of the day, Kettle One on the rocks.

I retrieved my cell phone and dialed Doc's number. It was almost lunch time, and even if he was working, I suspected that he would not be performing surgery with his back in spasms. As it turned out, he was on his patio when the phone rang having just returned home from his third and hopefully last treatment from Todd, his neighbor and Chiropractor.

Question: "Hi Doc, how're you feeling?"

Answer: "I'm feeling much better and think I'll be 100% by Monday. I'm going to relax this week-end. Too bad this happened just now; it would have been great to get away."

"Yep, we'll get another chance. Guess what….I'm going to get that rumored presidential appointment to the SEC. I'll be in Washington with W next week."

"Slow down. What's this all about?"

"It's a long story…..", but I had some time to kill. I recited the litany of players and events from Carlos to Russell to the Governor and on to the President as well as the new responsibilities and part-time geographic surroundings.

"Wow. Now, I'm really pissed off that this week-end didn't happen."

"Well, get your ass down here; you can still make it."

"I can't. I'm on the mend, but six hours on a plane would do me in."

"I was just kidding. Feel better. If we can, we'll get together on Tuesday either for lunch or dinner. We'll talk on Monday, if not sooner."

He concluded, "Have a ball."

I concluded, "How can I miss?"

My second beverage arrived as they updated the Departures Board with a new time: 3:00 PM. I was back to where I started and wound up, two hours to go. I would have just cleared Palm Beach airspace were it not for the delays and we took off in a timely manner. I removed the briefs prepared by Deborah on the SEC and our guest of honor, Ambassador Marine, and read each one thoroughly.

With only about half interest I watched the talking heads on CNBC providing Stock Market updates. Noting that we were having another Dow down day which would make the week a loser as well, I decided I had already experienced enough negativity for the day and changed my concentration back to the aircraft traffic and occasional putter.

With an hour to go, I glanced up at the board and damn it, they changed the time again for another hour's delay. That one really got to me. I walked over and spoke with a Delta ticket agent. How could the time keep changing? Where was the plane coming from? I was assured that the plane was already en route and would be arriving in just over an hour and be ready for the Vegas flight before two hours.

I went back to Sam Snead's and ordered my third drink. I was beginning to feel, but hopefully not speak, like Russell Savage. However, unlike my new buddy, I decided to have some lunch also. The Philly Cheese Steak was almost as good as those I have had in the City of Brotherly Love, but the scenery in Florida is much nicer than the northern competitor's.

As I swallowed my last bite, I observed a plane parking at gate A-3 and took a quick glace at the board confirming that it would only be forty-five minutes until my departure time. My glass was drained, the bill was paid and I made my way through the security checkpoints arriving at my designated gate with only half an hour until departure time. I knew that I was waitlisted for an upgrade to first class, but just then learned that I would have gotten the next available seat, if there were one, but there wasn't, so I didn't.

Delta Flight 711 to Las Vegas was ready for boarding at 3:45 PM By that time, I should have been thirty some odd thousand feet above Texas. Instead, we would just be boarding and arriving in Sin City around 6:30; a three hour delay.

For a brief instant I evaluated all the negatives of the day; Doc, the delay, not getting an upgrade and the buzz I had acquired at the lounge, in order to decide if I should call it a day and head home. Notwithstanding my seat in the back of the bus, I boarded with my fellow plebeians and braced myself for the next five plus hours.

Not to worry, I would have a movie or two to entertain me during the flight. At ten thousand feet, the flight attendant announced that the movie would be *Harry Potter and the Prisoner of Azkaban*. If I knew that prior to boarding, it might have skewed my decision into staying home. But since I did not have a parachute, I did the next best thing, walked to the flight attendant, requested two mini vodkas and some ice cubes. When I returned to my seat, I requested that Joe, the guy seated next to me, wake me as the Vegas skyline becomes visible.

Having received his assurances, I nursed the drink as I strategized my activities for the rest of the day. I would check in at Paris, freshen up in my room and go downstairs to Mon Ami Gabi, their outdoor restaurant on Las Vegas Boulevard, and order a garlic steak, get into a Vegas frame of mind with some people watching before entering the casino's chamber of chance. A double espresso would be the perfect closer, ensuring a few extra hours of playing time before slumber land called.

Moments later, I was sleeping. Poor Joe had to endure my snoring. It apparently was not much of a problem as he was already entrenched in Mr. Potter's adventures and paid little attention to my nasal trumpeting.

CHAPTER 14

FRIDAY AFTERNOON/EVENING

The final approach to McCarran International provides the neon splendor of an evening over Las Vegas Boulevard. It is perhaps the single best example of wasteful American energy utilization. Who cares, it is my Disneyworld! The Boeing 767 is my magic carpet floating over the Strip's version of several iconic destinations throughout the world. Oh, the Pyramids of Egypt, the distinct skyline of New York City, an ancient Grecian Forum, the Eiffel Tower, the canals of Venice and the Sahara Desert. Why go to EPCOT when all you have to do is visit Vegas?

One must traverse over a mile to get from the plane's jet-way to the luggage carousel. Fortunately, most of the journey is on a monorail tram, continuing with the Disneyworld metaphor. In the cavernous room housing the fourteen baggage roundabouts, Delta Flight 711 was relegated to carousel six just opposite the door to the taxi line and under a huge video monitor hawking Celine Dion's show at Caesars Palace.

When the buzzer sounds and the carousel starts turning, all travelers hope that they will win the suitcase derby having their bag arrive with the first salvo. Although it had happened in the past, such was not the case in that instance. The passengers still to be matched with their bags had winnowed down to five; I was among them. I was getting more furious by the moment. It would be my luck that the bag got lost, after all, the day had been going miserably and there was that acronym

DELTA – Don't Expect Luggage to Arrive. And, I felt as though I would scream, if I saw that purple floral bag go by me one more time before I got my bag,

My luggage was almost the last one off the carousel. It rounded third on its way home just as it was posted that Delta Flight 1274 from Denver's luggage was to be claimed on Carousel six. That obnoxious purple bag made three more laps before I retrieved mine and left; and still nobody was brave enough to claim ownership of such a hideous piece.

The baggage debacle was yet another omen piling on the negative events of the day, and still, I stayed rather than getting on the next plane back to paradise. Would good things ever triumph over the sour events I have had to endure thus far on this journey? Screw it, I was already in Vegas and shortly, I would be able to employ my considerable skills at the Blackjack Tables. Surely, my luck would change and the coming good times, just around the bend would overcome the setbacks that I had already encountered.

I entered the taxi queue: A mazelike walkway ultimately ending in a slot numbered one through twenty representing your designated cab. As I completed the line, I wound up at slot seven, but was instructed by the dispatcher to go to slot twenty. I assumed such decision was based on my ultimate destination or the fact that I was a single passenger. My chariot, one of Vegas' ubiquitous cabs arrived and I disclosed my destination, the Paris Hotel and Casino to the driver. We were off!

Paris' location, approximating mid-strip, and its ambience from its casino, to its shops, to its eateries, and yes, its rooms, give patrons the experience of actually being in the City of Lights. It is across the street from Bellagio and Caesars Palace and a short walk to any of the other top venues. It is my choice of where to stay in Vegas, hands-down.

Universally, cabbies are a breed unto themselves. However, those working in Vegas embody many characteristics indigenous only to Sin City. Rather than waiting for the hotel's Parisian café, my driver suggested that I start my escape immediately and offered me a drink. Who has a drink in a cab? I obviously noted that this was quite unusual and recognized that it would never have happened in Florida, but I was not in Kansas anymore and I accepted the cup. With hindsight and having the benefit of later reviewing the events as they unfolded, it was a dumb move. However, at the time I viewed such offering as a great way to start my weekend and scored it in the plus column. I thought that I was finally closing down on my running plus/minus count measuring the good and bad things thrust upon me since I left home this morning. I was wrong!

When in Vegas, I always judge my cab driver's character by his route selection exiting McCarran. The most direct route is to leave the airport via Paradise Road, past the University of Las Vegas and onto the strip. The alternative is via I-15, allegedly chosen to skip over the congested Strip traffic and more closely target the final destination. All cabbies that I have encountered have explained away the latter as a time saver to the passenger. I have always favored the more local route and felt that the Interstate just adds to the fare while bypassing the wonders of a Vegas night. Raul chose the Interstate and I finally gave up maintaining my good vs. bad score sheet.

The liquid I consumed in his cab was clear and tasted like vodka and even though it only filled half the plastic cup, it was obviously the strongest I ever consumed. It had the punch of a double or a triple, and seemed so much stronger. The radio was not playing, but I kept hearing repeating stanzas of the Beatles' "Lucy in the Sky with Diamonds."

While heading north on I-15, the strip is off to the east and you can easily see the significant symbols of each hotel. Not fully understanding the impact Raul's drink had on me, I was aware enough to notice that we just passed the Eiffel Tower; landmark to my hotel. Not even slowing down we just passed the circus tents and the iconic tower of the Stratosphere, the last hotels on the strip before the hiatus leading to the downtown casinos.

The driver was apparently on his own mission. He closed the Plexiglas partition between us and I heard the clicking evidence that he electronically locked my doors. Perhaps the most frustrating behavior was his refusal to talk. I could not even get a clue as to what lay ahead.

We exited onto the I-515 bypass and ultimately I saw a street sign on East Bonanza Street a few blocks north of the Downtown Strip, Freemont Street. He pulled into a Seven Eleven and before I knew what was happening, two guys jumped in the back doors, one from each side and slipped a hood over my head.

The situation was surreal, and quite scary. I was in a bad part of town. I had no idea of what these guys wanted from me. I already accepted that I would be robbed of my cash and the jewelry that I was wearing, but I was trying to keep my wits about me and stay alive. And, that was difficult given the effects of whatever it was that they had slipped into my drink.

The driving continued for several minutes before the taxi came to a stop. The three of us in the rear exited. However there were only two of us who knew what in the hell was going on and they were not going to share this information with me; at least not yet. I heard him give Raul the stipend for delivering me and instruct him to do as he was told.

The guy who paid off the Raul was the one who was seated to my left. Both of the new characters were careful not to speak in the cab and when I ultimately heard a voice it was from several feet away and hampered by the hood over my head and ears, and the street traffic. Although it was muffled, the voice did not sound completely unfamiliar. There was something that I could not quite put my finger on, but I knew that I had heard that voice before.

Other than recognizing that I was outdoors and within the environs of Las Vegas that few visitors experience, I was still clueless about my immediate future. Needless to say, Washington, D.C. was the last thing on my mind at that point of time.

I was sure that they had little intention of exposing either themselves or me, their hooded guest, to the outside world or any curious neighbors longer than was necessary. Accordingly, as soon as Raul pulled away, I was escorted, not gingerly, into an interior space. Was it a building, a residence or worse, a torture mill? Yes!

They shuffled me through my new prison. Other than the entry area, I counted two additional door openings before they stopped, instructed me to keep my eyes closed, removed my hood and my clothes and left me in complete darkness both literally and figuratively. Wanting to stay alive, I followed their instructions and kept my eyes closed until they left the room.

Apparently, the windows were darkened and my eyes adjusted to the near darkness illumined only by the narrowest of cracks along the bottom of a door. I was pleased to see that my area was a bedroom and not a customized fun area designed by the Marquis de Sade.

My abductors must have read *The Idiot's Guide to Kidnapping*; so far they could have been Poster Boys for the book. However, perfection is really quite rare and chinks in their armor were slowly unraveling. Dialogue, rather than soliloquies were heard through the door. It took only moments to learn that John was the guy who owned or otherwise controlled my current home. The question kept nagging me. Who was the other guy with whom he was speaking? And, clearly, it was the Mystery Man was the one calling the shots.

Slowly, my pupils adjusted and accommodated my curiosity providing the ability to gather more information. However, due to my handicap of darkness, the process was slow and in less detail than I would have desired. My cell contained a bed and a bureau/mirror combination completed by night stands on either side of a queen sized bed. The windows had plywood nailed over their openings and there were louvered doors leading into what I correctly assumed was a closet.

Just as I spied a wallet; my wallet sitting atop the dresser, reflected in the mirror, my minimal light was gone and the room went completely dark. John and his boss vacated the room adjacent to mine switching off the light. After, what seemed like an eternity, my eyes once again adjusted, as best they could, to the prevailing absence of light. I crawled on the floor towards the dresser. Upon reaching my destination, I felt my way up to the wallet and fondled it at length. I concluded with almost complete certainty that it was mine. I counted down to the third drawer and hid my bounty under the clothes stored on the right hand corner. How could they make such a colossal mistake as leaving my wallet so accessible?

If my theory relating to their incompetence was true, it was bolstered by finding clothing in that third drawer. I picked out what appeared to be a pair of shorts and a tee shirt and set my new ensemble just on top of my wallet. At first I only hoped that the colors were not orange and purple, or some such outrageous combination giving me the appearance of an indigent refugee if and when I ever freed myself of this incarceration. Ultimately, I realized that such was silly; I would have dressed like a circus clown in order get out of there.

Notwithstanding the potential peril I was facing, boredom still found a way to set in and I succumbed to the seduction of the bed. It had been at least twelve hours since I told Elaine that I loved her; and thankfully I took advantage of the opportunity; it might have been my last chance to do so. Should it be that I would not make it home alive, that moment would be the last entry in the *Ode to the Jewish Husband*; the posthumous "I love you," a final male attempt at laying guilt.

I was in a time warp and did not know if it was minutes or hours later when I was abruptly awakened. The two of them were in the room. The master yanked me out of bed, pinning my arms behind my back and his slave inserted a horse sized pill in my mouth and poured what felt like gallons on water down my throat ensuring its expeditious passage to where it would undoubtedly do the most harm.

They threw me back in the sack and quickly bolted for the crack of light; the door. The brief moment of opening allowed more light than I had seen in hours into the room thereby providing a momentary mental snapshot of both of my abductors. Even given its brevity, I was able to determine which of the two was John which added another level of intrigue into his superior's identity. The combination of his voice and brief appearance painted a clouded picture; one which I knew that I would eventually identify.

The pill was taking effect and I was out for the count.

CHAPTER 15

SATURDAY MORNING ????

I was awakened by a familiar sound; Was that a door chime? That was another clue; one supporting my conclusion that I was in a residence rather than a warehouse containing a rest area. My guess was that it was John's place. There were more voices becoming increasingly more understandable as they moved into the lighted room adjoining my cell. The new voices were those of females.

One of them asked "Which of you is David?"

Mystery Man replied, "the birthday boy is in the bedroom. He's gotten a little wasted, but we'll take some photos to make sure he remembers the party."

"It's a good thing that he called in yesterday with his credit card or my boss would not even let us come out. You guys will take care of the tip, right?"

"Of course, here's five hundred, give him a ride he'll always remember."

"How about if it's real special?

"O.K., you get another five if you make him smile. Listen, he's really gone, he may even put up a stink that he doesn't want to, but go on anyway. Let's get this show started."

"I know that he wants it, Mary told me how anxious he was on the phone yesterday."

Who in the hell was Mary? Recognizing that I only had a short time before the *fun* started, I tried to focus on logically processing all the data revealed so far. Those girls were not their friends and were not street hookers. Neither of those groups would accept credit cards for their services and they had a boss named Mary. They must have been from one of Vegas' countless escort services. But, I did not call to make these arrangements.

Mystery Man informed the ladies that they were going into the bedroom to get things ready and that they should undress and await the cue for their grand entrance. Simultaneously, the door opened and my two hosts entered the room. I heard the door to what I learned was a closet open and close. John flipped on the lights and was now fully visible. he was holding a camera and talking to his boss hidden in the closet observing through the louver doors, having removed one of the slats to improve his field of vision and yet still remain unseen. Why did they finally show an identity? And, why did Mystery Man remain so, by hiding in the closet?

The answer to the second question still nagged at me; it must be that I knew him. The answer to the first question became apparently clear as two naked beauties in their late twenties jumped into the bed with me as John started snapping away one voyeuristic shot after another.

The effects of the cocktail of liquids and pills that I ingested were stunning. My body seemed to be moving in slow motion, yet my mind was relatively alert. I felt as though I was on my "A" Game in working through the mosaic of clues presented. However, I knew that the dynamic duo would be joining me within seconds. I knew I had to resist, but strangely, I concurrently had what must have been a drug induced desire to go forward.

The thin girls introduced themselves as Nikki, the self imposed leader and Nora, "Hi Dave, we're gonna have a rodeo."

I grabbed Nikki, as though I was going to kiss her, and whispered in her ear "Where are you gals from?"

She planted a big one on me and whispered back, "Red Rock Escorts. Mary said she really enjoyed your call."

I noticed that even John was getting nervous about our banter; I could only imagine what Mystery Man was feeling. I had to devise a way to learn more from these girls; possibly an escape plan. Trying to accentuate my cerebral logical mind, I found myself fighting, but mostly yielding to the sensual devil in all of us. I mentally strapped myself in for what could be the ride of my life.

They grow them fast out there in Vegas! These girls had not yet celebrated their thirtieth birthdays, but they were solid professionals. The appetizer they served up was their mutual exploration of each other's body utilizing their tongues, their fingers, and a wide assortment of toys, some buzzing away while others were simply fluorescent. However, all of which were substantially larger than the toy I would soon introduce into the contest.

Even though they appeared to be doing fine without me, occasionally one or the other would direct my hand into a moist cave or direct my head to a breast desirous of some male attention. My mind already began the conversation with Elaine, "I couldn't help it, I was shanghaied. And besides, I only had my hand inside and a nip of a nipple." Maybe that would be my last thoughts of Elaine until this *ordeal* was over.

Not a chance! Anyone who knew the two of us, would know that such would never be the case. It was though she were there supervising the entire mission. Each time I had more than an observatory role and was called upon to participate, my rationalizations were amended to include all of the increasing acts I had performed. In the end, the list was so inclusive that all I could say to Elaine was "I love you, I never would have done it on my own, but I had no absolutely control over the situation."

Lest one think that it was only lust, I whispered another question to Nikki while Nora whispered to my Mr. Happy, who was getting happier by the minute, "What time is it?"

"David, don't you remember? I thought it weird that you wanted sex at 8:00 AM"

Is it weird to want sex at 8:00 AM? There was no need to upset my photographer by talking further. Notwithstanding the time of day or activities taking up that time, what I was going through was weird not an early libido.

Why was she seemingly familiar with me? She called me David or Dave on multiple occasions. And, either she or her boss, or both believed that I was the person arranging this little party. I needed more time for thinking without being pulled further into the dark side.

However, some things cannot be avoided. One cannot stop a volcano from erupting. And, so it was with our party: The crescendo, the climax, the end; it came.

John was snapping away at a furious clip as Nikki lifted her head wiping my smile off her face while Nora looked on from her perch upon my head, which was not recognizable as only my nose and mouth were visible. She proudly requested, "How was that, do we get extra five hundred?"

"O.K. ladies, you earned it, he won't forget you" John replied. "Go get dressed and I'll drop you off out west."

As they departed, he turned the light off and as though on queue, Mystery Man left the closet. As he opened the door to the adjoining room, the light behind him silhouetted his face and gave me a glimpse of his eyes which were staring at me, a scary, but somewhat familiar sight. I was sure that the boss thought that John provided way too much information to me; of course he did. "You were right; pictures are better than if we would've recorded a video."

It was the master who initiated their departure, not wanting to have to speak too much in my presence. Outside he chided "John, you speak too much." Although, in this case, he was correct. A video would reveal many instances where I was less than enthusiastic, almost protesting; not quite the image that they would prefer to show to whomever was on their intended distribution list. The hundreds of snaps I heard could easily be distilled down to a dozen or more that would provide all the embarrassment I could endure.

It was a given that Elaine would be involved in *the who to* equation, but the question was where else would the photographs go? One or two sent to the White House would immediately derail my position in Washington. A blanket e-mail to partners and employees of my firm would create a seismic event disrupting workflow for months, perhaps forever.

The silence was broken with Nikki saying "Thanks guys, don't forget to give David a good-bye kiss from us."

From John, "I'm out of here. I've got a couple of errands to run after I drop the ladies off. I'll be home way before you need me."

Mystery Man's cell phone rang and he reflexively answered before the second ring. "Hi dad." He was obviously moving into the other room as the voice, and my ability to hear it dwindled. "Yeah, things are going great." A pause for his dad's response, and then "yes tonight….." was the last words I could discern.

I was alone again and adjusting to the darkness. My mind was racing, taking inventory of what I knew and what I feared, and constantly trying to utilize these to unravel more layers of the puzzle. I surmised that it was late morning approaching noon. My body and movements still felt sluggish and I knew that the drugs were still impacting my thought process.

John was gone. He was driving the girls somewhere west of my current location somewhere in the vicinity of the downtown strip. Nikki responded Red Rock Escorts; its offices were probably on West Charleston on the way to the namesake, Red Rock Valley. The conclusion: I would be alone with the Mystery Man for at least two hours before John returned.

I got dressed in the shorts and tee shirt that I stashed away yesterday, retrieved my wallet and crawled into the closet finding a pair of flip flops. Like a hunting lion, I haunched down on my knees with my ears flat against the door. I had to learn more. There appeared to be a prolonged period of silence. Fully expecting to find the door locked as was the case last time I checked, it was unlocked. Apparently the Whiz Kid, John, forgot to lock it when he left.

I was now in the adjoining area, not a room, but a hallway with four doors; presumably a bathroom and two additional bedrooms. The closed door to one of the rooms displayed a beam of light from within; presumably the bathroom accommodating the needs of Mystery Man.

Assuming I was correct, I bolted out of that area through a great room into the kitchen where I saw a set of keys hanging from a hook by the door. But more importantly, I also noticed a camera attached by a wire to a computer. Instinctively, I grabbed the keys and the camera and ran outside to the driveway searching for the right key to open my jackpot; a waiting car and an escape.

It was a Chevy that looked like it was a decade old, but at that point, it was a luxury vehicle and all that I could have asked for. I was four blocks away before it dawned on me that I should have at least written down the address or looked at a street sign before now. Retracing my route was not an option. At that juncture I was indeed on Freemont Street, confirming my reasoning about the general area in which I was held captive.

I was free; or was I?

CHAPTER 16

SATURDAY AFTERNOON

The clock on the dashboard flashed 1:15. Assuming that was correct, it was 1:15 PM on Saturday. I could not confirm that data, as they did keep my Rolex. Upset about that, I was comforted by knowing that they did not take my pinky ring. It was a gift from my father on my eighteenth birthday, originally gifted to him by his dad, the original David Atlas, patriarch of the family.

I did not have dad's portrait to talk to and provide logical assistance and comfort as I progressed through my malaise, but I felt that he would have been proud of my ability to keep my head in the game, in more ways than one, and yet surface to freedom.

Without patting myself too heavily on my back, I had to objectively admit that it really was quite easy to escape. And, they did give me a few significant clues to be able to drill down to learn more about this escapade. I drove south towards my safety zone, the strip looking for an appropriate area to stop, regroup and develop a strategy for what I would do next.

I assumed that, although I had the camera, the pictures were already downloaded to the computer to which it was connected. Why did I not grab the computer also, or at least disable its hard drive containing the copies of my photographs. Why? Because I wanted to get the hell out of there and did not have the benefit of solid thinking. And, now I did not even know the address.

If possible I had to retrieve the original digital images. Surely they would make their way to Elaine who would inexorably find them difficult to accept. My thoughts were interrupted by a flashing yellow light indicating the absence of gasoline. Coincidently, I was coming upon a gas station which was adjacent to a retail strip center featuring Lorenzo's Fashions.

I pulled into the station and removed my wallet from my rear hip pocket. In my haste to leave, I never checked to see if it was in fact, my wallet. I removed my driver's license and once again thanked them for my good fortune. Finding any measure of good fortune in my saga was purely ironic. However, this was Las Vegas and I expected nothing but good fortune for this week-end.

Recognizing that I had to get rid of my current ride fairly soon, I filled it up anyway at the self-service pump and used the American Express card behind my license. I then pulled into the retail mall in front of the male haberdashery. I also needed to get out of my current duds; I looked like an indigent Conch from Key West.

I purchased two pairs of khakis, two collared shirts, underwear, socks and a pair of topsiders. I would not make the cover of Gentlemen's Quarterly but, notwithstanding what I had just undergone, at least I look civilized.

While in the fitting room, it was fitting to use the time to evaluate my next move. I decided that I had to get a car that my captors would not be familiar with. Accordingly, I decided my next move was to go to the Stratosphere. I could see its space needle projecting into the skyline, a mere four blocks away. Budget Car Rentals, not usually my carrier of choice, had a satellite office in the hotel.

I settled the clothing tab with the same American Express card; *don't leave home without it*, grabbed my new wardrobe and headed to my temporary car en route to make a vehicular switch.

As I inserted the key into the door, I noticed four Las Vegas Police Officers approaching me with instructions to place my hands on the roof of the car. In seconds my hands were placed behind my back and plastic hand restraints were tightened about my wrists. They turned me around and indicated that I was being placed under arrest for driving a stolen vehicle, and although they went on with a list of other infractions, I did not listen because in a parked van, three spaces away I once again saw that stare that I could not place: Mystery Man. He was hiding under the brim of a hat and adorning facial hair in the form of a mustache and goatee, but there was no doubt that it was him.

I was again headed downtown, once again in the backseat of a vehicle; this time albeit a "paddy wagon" taking me to a place that I had no desire to be. This time however, the site was at least disclosed to me; the Clark County Detention Center. I had passed this facility several times in past years, never giving a second thought as to its purpose or that it would at some time factor into my life.

Pulling into the underground garage, I noticed that we were a stone's throw from the famed, Golden Nugget Hotel and Casino. Seeing the casino made me reflect that I could not recall ever being in Vegas that long without making a wager. Things were different this time, gaming was the last thing on my mind. However, the stakes I was now playing with were the richest that I have ever ventured.

My wallet, jewelry and *camera* were inventoried and I learned the full extent of my problems as I was processed like a common criminal. In the eyes of Sergeant Alan Cooper I was a common criminal. I was charged with driving a stolen vehicle and fraudulently using stolen credit cards. It was stupid of me to just check my license to ensure it was my wallet, while not checking the credit cards.

Upon completing the obligatory photo and fingerprinting session, I learned that another infraction would be added to those that I already had to defend. My blood-alcohol level was over the limit and traces of drugs were found in my urine, adding charges of driving under the influence to my multitude problems.

The interrogation was short as I immediately indicated that I wanted counsel. They departed while I placed a call to my partner, Ed Sheerson. I caught him on the eighth hole of his community's golf course, whereupon he excused himself and ferreted out the assistance that I required.

He assured me that he would engage a local attorney to assist with the charges I would be facing and that he would do so as expeditiously as possible. Further, he let me know that he viewed engaging a private investigator in Las Vegas as a top priority. Ed concluded with his promise that he would be on the next flight out to offer additional support.

Having completed my call, Cooper and his henchman moved me into a holding cell already home away from home for two reprobates; my new roommates for who knew how long. Perhaps I should not have reached such a quick conclusion about my roomies.

Three Finger Lonnie earned his name for the obvious reason. I hoped that I would not be there long enough to ask him how he lost the other two. Lonny was a third rate hustler. He was no real threat to society unless you were unfortunate to fall prey to one of his street scams, and even if one did, his losses would be in the twenty – forty dollar range; penny ante compared to the city's real threats. I learned that he was a fairly regular visitor to our current hostel.

My other friend did warrant the quick evaluation. He was a real scumbag and I did my best to avoid him at all costs. He was arrested for raping his neighbor. All he offered us in his defense was that she wanted it, she asked for it and she loved it; until her husband caught them and she yelled rape at top of her lungs. I made another rapid judgment, Reggie was guilty as sin; no one would want to make love with that guy.

This was turning out to be one hell of a week-end, and apparently it was not over yet. Although this time I knew where I was, I was not sure that I was better off in my current circumstance than I was in the last. All else being equal, I still had Nikki and Nora to keep my mind off of reality and give me some clues to move forward. This certainly would not be the case with my Moe and Larry, Lonnie and Reggie.

I would love to say that we wiled away the hours having cocktails and playing bridge, but such was not the case. My conversation was almost entirely concentrated with my new three indexed buddy. I concluded that Lonny was an unfortunate soul who just needed a break; fundamentally a poor guy down on his luck. Did I get conned again?

Reggie was, and is the low life I initially pegged him as being. Not only would I not want him be alone with any woman I cared about, I tried not to let him be alone with me. My mind had visions of Bubba telling me how much he loved me.

If it were not for the surroundings, I would have enjoyed Lonnie's company much more. He was most charming and disclosed that he had been in Vegas since the Rat Pack days. He must have been just a kid, because he was not much older than me. The stories were nostalgic and almost let me forget where I was. Such was my bridge game! I knew he was conning me on some level, but it was mindless and passed the time until our arraignment. Moreover, it kept my dealings with Reggie to a minimum.

Thanks Doc, thanks Randall, thanks Mr. President and a special thanks to you, Susan for making my trip possible in the first place. It is a natural reaction to blame others as one's reaction to unpleasant events. I had to stop playing the blame game. I was boiling in the soup and it was up to me to get out and lower the flame.

The steel door separating the holding cells from quasi-freedom creaked open and I saw a man in a suit enter; a good sign, asking "Which of you is David Atlas?"

Eureka, my *Get Out of JailFree* card! "I am...... I am," I screeched like an eager child.

Speaking to his escort, "Please release my client. We have a lot to talk about." Speaking to me "Hello, I'm Jerome Goldstein, your partner Ed Sheerson arranged for me to be here."

Although I should not have been surprised, I was pleased, at least temporarily, as we were offered a change of venue, a conference room. It offered much more civilized surroundings and the promise of moving closer to the front door. Aside from the fact that no bars were visible and that the room lacked the noxious essence of urine, I was still not free. However, now I was with someone who was going to hopefully get me through this long nightmare and it was a most welcomed retreat from my previous parlor.

Jerome....Jerry gave me an oral rendition of his *Curriculum Vitae*. He was a recognized criminal attorney with his office in a commerce-center out by the airport: The high rent district. After learning of his background, I determined that resume would have been fine but I could have skipped the Latin. Notwithstanding, I was confident that he would be able to bail me out.

He went on, "Ed gave me some of the facts and I have read the Police Report. What's your end of it?"

There was no need to retell the saga from Miss Fox or my partners' trivialities; my life, *ad nauseam*. Accordingly, I picked up the events from Raul picking me up at McCarran. I tried to be as specific as possible recognizing that little gems may be hidden in obscure observations and could possibly be discerned by another mind. In addition, I went into some enhanced detail with respect to Nikki and Nora; not quite sure if I was attempting to be informative or just bragging. I concluded with, "So? What do you think? When do I get out of this place and then what?"

"Judge Harlan is wonderful; he convenes at 6:00 PM everyday, weekends included. You'll be out of here by 7:00, but we've got a lot of work to do. Ed also engaged a Private Investigator, Fast Eddie Seng. We'll meet with him for breakfast tomorrow and work out a game plan."

Fast Eddie... this whole thing was taking on a Damon Runyon aura. "Jerry, this is my life, why wait until morning? I'm not going to be playing blackjack tonight."

"We need to get you in a room, get you a computer and pour over the events in detail. You and I will be busy until Ed and Eddie get here."

"Ed's a stand-up guy. What time does he get here?"

"He's going to call from Palm Beach as soon as he gets confirmed, but he should be here by 9:30 in the morning."

"You keep telling me about our evening, when do we bust out?"

Looking at his watch, he replies, "It is six o'clock, and we should get the nod any moment now."

Jerry knocked on the window signaling that our meeting was concluded. The guard indicated that he was just on his way to get us for our appearance before the alliteratively Honorable Harlan H. Harlan; a man whose parents apparently lacked any originality. I was afraid to ask what the H. stood for.

The judge appeared to be a fair guy. Although it was not entirely necessary, he sufficiently informed me of the seriousness of the charges, my responsibilities and the penalties associated with noncompliance. Recognizing that I still had a serious mountain of crap that I had to climb, I was required to pledge $100,000 to gain my freedom; my second escape for the day.

I retrieved my personal belongings, including the *camera* and sought refuge in Jerry's Lexus. Saturday was one hell of a day.

I knew not what horrors awaited me?

CHAPTER 17

SATURDAY EVENING

I needed several things, but my initial request was a reasonably sterile bathroom. I feared what my body would have been subjected to if I had used the facilities at the detention center. Jerry pulled into the parking lot of a local steak house and we entered the restaurant providing me the opportunity to rejoin the human race.

I freshened up in the men's room utilizing three towels handed to me individually by the attendant. Not only was I confident that I adequately cleaned myself, I was equally sure that I did not have any money to tip my valet. I assured him that I would return with his reward momentarily. I explained, and Jerry handed me $200 in assorted bills. True to my word, I returned with a Russell Savage sized twenty dollar reward. One does strange things when one is out on bail.

The steaks were wonderful, not like the one I told Doc I would be having at Paris' Mon Ami Gabi, but much better than my last meal, a Philly Cheese steak at Palm Beach International. I did however refrain from any alcohol; my head and body were finally getting clear from the effects of the various drugs plied on me since arriving here.

Jerry presented a full accounting of the charges I was facing. Driving under the influence is serious, but all we had to do was prove my abduction, surely no judge would hold me culpable for escaping before waiting for the drugs and booze to ebb. Once the truth was known, it would also absolve me of using fake credit cards planted in my wallet by the thugs.

As we left the restaurant, I noticed an Office Depot across the street and I needed a computer and some supplies. I told Jerry that I could use the fresh air and exercise and that I would walk over; he could move the car and meet me inside. We were just a few blocks off the strip, but we could have been in most hometowns, USA; everyday people going about their everyday chores. I was the exception; I was on a mission to save my freedom, my marriage, my career…my life.

I made the requisite purchases with a credit card provided by Jerry. I suspected that I would never again use plastic without first looking at the name embossed thereon. Before leaving I went over the mental checklist of items I would need for some internet research and note taking. I had to get to the bottom of this and I would prefer to do so before Tuesday's Red-eye to PBI.

The truth was hidden below the layers of knotted deceit foisted upon me and appeared to be Georgian to unravel. I had interpersonal contact with very few individuals since arriving in Vegas; Raul, John and the Mystery Man. Nikki and Nora were in a different class, but surprisingly served up the first clue, a chink in the armor housing the secrets of my saga.

Nikki had disclosed to me that I arranged our party through her employer, Red Rock Escorts. Further the owner, or at least manager, Mary had a conversation with me. I knew that a conversation with me was bogus, but I determined that it would be necessary for me or one of my minions to have a conversation with her.

Coming upon a Walgreens, I asked Jerry to pull in allowing me the opportunity to secure some required toiletries. I did not want to waste time and while I was checking out, I noticed Jerry going through a phone book and ultimately writing something down on a business card.

When we were in the car he handed me his cell phone and the business card, "it's an escort service and it's only 9:00 PM, somebody might answer."

I dialed the number on Jerry's cell phone. It was answered, "Red Rock Escorts, Mary speaking." Bingo!

"Hi Mary, this is David Atlas" hoping to get a friendly response.

"Hi David, how did you enjoy your wake-up call?"

Playing along, "it was great, but I've got a few questions. When and where did you speak to me last?"

"You called me from your office in Florida on Thursday morning. Are you O.K.?"

"I'm fine, I just want to confirm a few things. Nikki said that I had already paid you. Which credit card did I use?"

She recited my Atlas, Immerson and Sheering American Express number and anticipated my next question, "And, yes your firm name came up on the caller I.D. You're not trying to deny the charge, are you?"

"No, no….Can you reach Nikki or Nora, I would love to see them again."

"Oh that's a relief. I hate it when phone-ins try to claim their meeting never took place. The strange thing is that I haven't heard from them since they met with you this morning. Can I reach you on this number when they call in?"

"Yes and thank you. You've been very helpful."

Jerry added to me "Thank you. That information was very helpful."

"Now we know that somebody in your office made the call. You're being set up on your own home court," was the logical response he offered.

Of course, he was correct!

Modern technology is wonderful. I made a call from a cell phone in Las Vegas on a Saturday evening and ascertained that either I was nuts or a conspiracy reaching from West Palm Beach to Nevada is seeking to ruin my life. I knew that I never placed that call, but apparently somebody did; someone who knew about my itinerary and had access to the firm's credit card number. However, it added another layer to my problems to replace the one that we just uncovered.

Not wanting to be close to the seductive draw of a casino and at Jerry's suggestion, I checked into the Vagabond Motel which was located halfway between the main and downtown strips. Although not French Provincial in its ambience, it was clean, offered free internet and provided sufficient anonymity to allow me what I truly needed; a good night's rest. He joined me in the inspection of *my suite*; he did not want to leave until he was sure that I was settled for the evening.

Acknowledging my acceptance of the accommodations, I suggested we go over a few nagging thoughts before he left. Jerry was either very bright or extremely intuitive, or both; he listed them in my order of priority.

How were the girls arranged from my office, presumably by me?

Who were my abductors and where did they take me?

Who was Tomas Calvo who claimed that I robbed his car? Was it his house that I was held captive? Why was his car there?

Why was this happening to me... .and, why now?

Most importantly, how can I get this all resolved by Monday?

Jerry initiated the departure emphasizing that I needed to get some sleep. Of course, he was correct. He indicated that he would call my room in the morning as soon as he hooked up with our investigator, Fast Eddie. How could I possibly forget, *Fast Eddie;* I really was in the Twilight Zone. We would either meet at the hotel or he would send a taxi to bring me to his office. Please, not another taxi!

I was alone within the four walls of my new cell. In a frenzy, I eagerly unwrapped and set up my new laptop, booting it up as expeditiously as possible. The familiar Windows sign-on chimed and I was off. Internet access was available and speedy; the photo card from the camera fit into the appropriate slot on the laptop and I already had access to John's masterful portfolio.

I knew that I could spend hours with my new toy, but fatigue was rapidly conquering a questioning mind. Curiosity prevailed at least one more time. I did a Google search on Tomas Calvo who owned the car in which I was arrested while escaping what I thought was my nightmare.

The only plausible Calvo match listed an address west of the Interstate and miles south of where I was deposited after being kidnapped. The other possibility, a T. Calvo was an architect way out west and he did not appear to fit in the existing Rogue's Gallery. I shut down the computer and made my way to the bathroom.

Somewhere between showering and brushing my teeth, the recurring questions and images nagged at me. Who was doing this to me and why? The staring eyes of Mystery Man ominously projected into my mind. Who in the hell was he?

I was closing the light in the bathroom alcove, and the 11:00 O'clock News broke into its weather segment; such was my background noise. Not really caring about Nevada's unusually warm September, I was only paying partial attention to the tube when the broadcaster turned national in scope and reported that Hurricane Misty, a late and unpredicted storm was wrecking havoc in the Caribbean. She had sprung up from nowhere and had the National Hurricane Center in Miami facing the nation with egg on their tanned, or was it reddened, face.

This brought a whole new meaning to the Perfect Storm. I was fighting the elements in the desert and who knew what Elaine was going through in the tropics. What else could possibly go wrong?

CHAPTER 18

SATURDAY EVENING

I kept asking myself how all this shit could be happening to me, and then came along of all things a hurricane, one with which Elaine would have to endure without me. Elaine and I spent a harrowing night at my Aunt Bea's house in Miami during Hurricane Andrew and neither of us would want to face another.

The local news was informative in that it alerted me to a serious matter, but lacking the specificity that I desired. The tracking path, its intensity and anticipated timing were all questions in my mind. I tried to recall any mention of the brewing storm while viewing Thursday's evening news when I remembered that we did not watch it to the end; Elaine was amorous and shut it off and turned me on. Given all the circumstance we were both facing, that was a welcomed picture in my mind.

While my new laptop was booting up, I recalled that August evening twelve years ago as Andrew tore through South Miami.

All of Florida was tracking Hurricane Andrew's progress for days. It was a classical storm intensifying at predictable times and traveling exactly as projected by the National Hurricane Center. It hit Cuba and the Bahamas exactly at the time, location and intensity predicted by the experts and it was headed toward southeast Florida with a projected land fall in Fort Lauderdale during the afternoon or early evening of August 24, 1992.

The day before, Sunday, we tidied up the patio bringing inside all furnishings and accessories which could become missiles. We were north of the expected storm path through Florida, but recognized that it would still be windy. Many locals, especially the carpetbaggers from the north, like Elaine and I, had never experienced a hurricane and were too complacent about its potential wrath.

Such were our storm preparations. Southeast Florida had not seen a significant storm in decades and although Hurricane Andrew was a big one, it had followed the experts' tracking models and all were confident that it would make landfall in Broward County sometime Monday afternoon. We had pop corn and cable, we were all set.

We were watching Sixty Minutes when I received a call from my Aunt Beatrice. She still lived in South Florida and asked if I would please bring her to our home to ride out Andrew. She was as far south of its projected path as we were north, but our home and its residents were younger and better able to weather a storm. Besides, she did not like being alone.

I assured her that either Michael or Elaine and I would be there mid-morning and wanted to immediately head back to Boca. She should pack enough for her needs and Rusty's, her black mutt of over a decade, for a few days. Michael, who was home that week-end and not pre-warned of those arrangements, protested. We acquiesced to providing the chauffeuring services and requested that he delay his return to Tampa until the storm passed.

Minutes later Michael left to pick up his friend Chad for their evening's delights leaving us alone in our house. Although Aunt Bea was important in my life providing me my scholarship for college, I tuned her along with the coming hurricane out of my mind replaced by more intimate thoughts of Elaine. Our evening was great; so great that we slept in on Monday.

That Monday morning, we had a quick cup of coffee and headed south toward Miami to retrieve my aunt and her canine pal. Although we had originally planned on being there by 11:00, it was about then when we started the hour plus drive, each way. In the car, I called my aunt and Ed Sheerson to confirm that we were en route and, to inform

Ed that Michael would be home alone if we were detained in Miami. How prophetic!

We arrived at Aunt Bea's house and were greeted with a note pinned to the front door, "Gone to get Rusty, be back soon." I did not know if the message was two minutes or an hour old, nor was I familiar with her definition of soon.

Should she get back soon, she would be greeted with a note bearing our response, "Gone to Panera's to pick up some sandwiches, it's now 12:45; see you soon."

We were back at her house in about forty minutes and there was still no sign of her. Not having a key to the house, we backed into her driveway and ate our sandwiches awaiting her return. We finished our feast and began contemplating if we should share her turkey wrap also, when I thought about going next door to see if they knew her cell phone number, or where she was for that matter.

No, they did not know her cell phone, but yes, they knew where she was. Well, sort of knew where she was. They informed me that apparently Rusty broke free from the backyard sometime last night and that she was driving the neighborhood looking for him. Wonderful! I loved the specificity of their input, it provided so much insight in determining our next move; a quick sweep of the neighborhood and extended surveillance from her driveway.

By 3:00 I was getting frantic and decided to go off on another sweep leaving Elaine stationed at the house holding down the fort. At 3:45 my cell rang and Elaine confirmed all was well with my aunt and her wayward dog. I returned to her house to find them huddled around the television and shaking.

Andrew had made a last minute turn to the south and our house appeared to be another dot on its predicted path. "Let's get the hell out of here," I yelled.

Elaine replied "They just showed aerials over the turnpike and I-95; they're parking lots."

Usually the leader, I asked, "Where can we go?"

Elaine, the designated leader replied, "We're here!"

"Did you call Michael?"

She was a step ahead of me, "Yes, Ed already called him and he'll be at their house until we get home."

"Again, I was relegated to the role of errand boy, I'm going back to Panera's. Do you need anything else, Aunt Bea?"

"Yeah, pick up some batteries, flash lights, candles…"

Getting more upset by the minute and not up to date on my short-hand skills, I asked sarcastically, "Wait a minute, do you have a Home Depot Checklist?" They both shot me *THE LOOK*, a piercing stare suggesting the husband was on the thinnest of ice and facing untold retribution from the wife; a phenomenon discussed at length in the *Ode to the Jewish Husband*. Without uttering another word, I left for my errands. We still had a few hours before the winds would get there.

I returned with the requisite hardware and food provisions to get us through the evening anticipating our departure some time in the early morning hours after the storm had passed. As the only thing being televised was hurricane related, we watched hurricane related stories and the warnings were getting more ominous by the minute, until we lost electricity and went back to those radio days of yesteryear.

Man, women and beast were safely huddled in a hallway with all doors to adjoining rooms closed. Growing weary of the candlelight and crackling radio, and still anticipating our departure as soon as the *all clear Signal* was given; the storm's passing, I decided to attempt some sleep.

I got my wake-up call around midnight when the front door was breached and crashed open. The change in pressure combined with gusting winds and flying missiles proved too much for each window in the house. The pummeling wind and rain freed the windows from their housing causing them to crash inward, often two or three at a time.

Not feeling secure, we sought what was thought to be the next best bunker: The laundry room; an interior space with no windows. That feeling of security lasted until the garage door blew in causing the wall it shared with the laundry room to shake in rhythm and intensity with the wind.

The house was not safe. The sudden change in air pressure caused by the front door blowing in sent the roof over my aunt's bedroom flying off to Oz. We knew that there was glass and debris all over the house and walking around was dangerous. After what seemed like an eternity, but only about an hour, we hung out our white flag and took refuge in a bathtub with a mattress over us; our last line of defense.

Happily leaving my horrific memories of Andrew, I noticed that the computer was ready to go. I Googled Hurricane Misty. Where in the hell did they come up with that name? I would not have been surprised if the first internet hit was for a nude dancer in Vegas.

Hurricane Misty was the thirteenth named storm of the 2004 hurricane season; the Vegas metaphors continued with an unlucky thirteen. She was first noticed as a tropical storm off the coast of Africa almost two weeks ago and, although moving on a predicable path, she did not significantly take the shape or the concern of a hurricane until she was off the coast of Haiti on Thursday morning. And then, all hell broke loose!

It ravaged the eastern half of Cuba and shortly thereafter maintained a path towards the Bahamas as a Category Three or Four Storm with sustained winds of 110 miles per hour. I could not recall if Nassau was stop one or two on Elaine's cruise. I could not even recall the ship that they were on, but I knew that it was a Carnival sailing. Accordingly, the next site that I keyed in was Carnival.com

Their home page was user friendly and had an easy link to Hurricane Misty questions. The introductory sentence to the introductory paragraph was a calm port in one hell of a storm, Elaine was on their ship in unaffected waters; smooth sailing. The ship had changed its itinerary to avoid the storm and the extended northeasterly cruise would also extend the girls' return. They would disembark in Fort Lauderdale on Tuesday evening. At least I had a few additional hours to set things straight.

I did so hope to be there to greet them with the Vegas nonsense behind me, but there were still too many unanswered questions and "............miles to go before I sleep."

Notwithstanding, I went to sleep.

CHAPTER 19

SUNDAY MORNING

Refreshed, showered and coffeed courtesy of the in-room coffee-maker, I booted up the computer and awaited the call from Jerry and Fast Eddie Seng.

It was 8:15 AM when I turned on the television for background noise and got on the computer. The local news was in its five minute local update break from the network morning show. The temperature would be in the mid-seventies. Good, I did not want to go swimming anyway. The anchor announced that there was breaking news and turned the story over to one of their staff reporters in the downtown area. It appeared that an overnight fire destroyed a house killing its owner, Juan Alvarez, who was sleeping through the ordeal. There were signs of arson and the Las Vegas Fire and Police Departments were conducting investigations.

I heard the report, but it did not register. I probably could repeat the salient points of the story. However, I did not see the nexus to me until later in the day. I was busily reviewing the gallery of photographs that John was kind enough to leave in his camera. I was hopeful that the camera contained the only copies of those images, but was confident that another set existed on his computer. At least I understood what I was up against. Clearly, these guys thought this adventure through. Their planning was excellent, but there were many gaps in their execution. Both the guys and the girls were beauties; albeit for different reasons.

My first lap around the track of pictures was at a fast clip in order to quickly ascertain how much trouble I would be in when Elaine had her chance to do the same. I suspected that her pace would be much slower and with a completely different set of emotions. My second viewing was almost voyeuristically slow, but not for that reason. I was focused on background images trying to obtain further clues.

The phone rang and Jerry revealed that he and Fast Eddie were at the airport picking up Ed Sheerson who arrived five minutes ago and that they would be joining me in approximately twenty minutes at the hotel. Further, he wanted to meet in my room for a few minutes before leaving to grab breakfast.

Having a solid twenty minutes, I returned to John's photographic handiwork. He shot his pictures from every imaginable angle. Accordingly, the portfolio, in its entirety, also provided background shots of the walls all around the room. The covered windows, the furnishings and the missing slat with two peering eyes were confirmed. Nothing new unfolded, until the money shot.

Unfortunately the one photo providing proof that the girls had worked their magic and earned their bonus, was the same one which served up a valuable clue. Most eyes would be on her face, but just beyond her was a mirror with a reflection of the photographer's face partially visible, although somewhat blocked by the camera. Thankfully, he shot many photos in rapid succession changing eyes and camera angle from time to time. That sequence, six shots in all, provided the full image of his face, but in different pieces.

I copied those six photographs into separate files in order to have someone work through either *Photo Shop* or a more advanced editing software to pull together a full picture of John's face. We had a jigsaw puzzle of John's identity.

A knock on the door reminded me that I was expecting company. Jerry, Ed Sheerson and Fast Eddie Seng entered my room. While Ed offered me a brotherly hug and assurances that the Hurricane was a non-issue to Elaine, Jerry deposited the Sunday *Las Vegas Review-Journal* on my bed and the Fast Man waited his turn for an introduction.

Seng, was in his full sartorial splendor of shorts and a Hawaiian surfing shirt, and was working through his sales pitch including several examples of the wonders he had provided for clients in the past. Except for wardrobe, it reminded me of my first meeting with Barry Vincent, where my sales effort was also not necessary. There also the engagement was solely predicated on the referral source. In this case, all he needed was Jerry's endorsement, which apparently he had.

Not wanting, but unable to avoid cutting his presentation short, I glanced at the lead sheet of the newspaper lying on my bed and saw John's photo. The story was about the fire; the one reported on the news earlier, but with greater specificity. I learned that my John was the Juan Alvarez who owned and died in the house that was burned down last evening. And, the authorities believed that it was a homicide.

I opened the picture folder saved in the computer and shared them with the gang reminding them that the focus should be on the mirror and not on the action in the foreground. Although I faced both kudos and fraternal jabs from the boys, the end result was undeniable; John, a.k.a. Juan Alvarez was involved with both my abduction and party. We had to be prepared for questions from the police.

Picking up the paper and pointing at John's face, I incredulously asked "How is it possible that one of the guys who abducted me winds up dead?"

Jerry had to ask the question, but did so as delicately as possible "Did you go to sleep and stay in the room after I left?"

"Yes, I was in my room all night. You don't think I did it. Do you? I don't even know the address."

"No, but the police might and we need some answers." Either hoping, against hope or just feigning humor "Were Nikki or Nora, or both here with you?"

If I were not so scared, I would be pissed off with his remark. In fact, I was pissed off! "What the hell's wrong with you?"

"Calm down. I know that you didn't do it. Let's get some breakfast."

I concluded "Who could eat, I'm not hungry?"

I found out that no matter what the problems are one could probably eat. I downed enough to warrant a verbal barrage from Elaine if she witnessed my meal. However, I had other issues to deal with that were more pressing than my wife's menu for my life. Notwithstanding my thoughts of Elaine and the rain cloud seeded above me, breakfast proceeded in a relatively light and casual fashion. It was not until we returned to my room that things got focused and frightful.

Sergeant Cooper at the Clark County Detention Center took my statement at the time of my arrest. Although I told him the general vicinity of my earlier detention, I did not know the actual address. Of course, it would be logical for him to expect an escapee would look at the address or at least street name, at the corner, upon achieving an escape. However, I did not do so and, the burnt abode was the site of my captivity.

The boys convinced me that the victory in finding one of my captors, which supported the saga of my being shanghaied, was *only* one side of the story. The photographs also provided a strong motive for me wanting to get even and although the fire was terrible for Juan Alvarez, it was not good for me either. My alibi was weak; mostly self-serving and probably not capable of outweighing the other presumptions.

Eddie asked Ed a few questions out of my earshot and shortly thereafter retreated outside as Ed pulled out his cell phone. Jerry and I focused on the charges against me and the most current event, John's death. I found it difficult to adjust to the new status quo. I was euphoric upon establishing John as one of the culprits only to find that I would be implicated in his death.

As though on cue, Jerry decided to go back to basics and commenced with, "I know that you are familiar with the charges against you, but let's go over each one with the added information that we now have." He reiterated that success on the DUI count was entirely linked to proving the abduction and although it did not completely defend the utilization of stolen identity and credit cards, it made the defense much easier. Solving the mystery of Mystery Man remained at the fulcrum of my success.

Goldstein hands me an enlarged photocopy of a Nevada Driver's License. Without looking at the name and address, I flip it back to him with, "How did you find Raul so quickly?"

The license was issued to a Tomas Calvo and he responded, "This is the guy who owned the car you were driving. Why'd you call him Raul?"

I responded, "He was the taxi driver who brought me to this Hell." At least, according to the credentials in his cab, he was Raul, Raul Garcia licensed by the state of Nevada to drive for Southwest Desert Taxi.

Recognizing that I could not answer the question, he rhetorically asked "What's his connection to Alvarez or the other guy?"

Figuring that one out was clearly beyond me at that time. I pulled rank and added, "I thought that's why we have a guy like Fast Eddie. By the way, where is he?"

"Yes, he's going to work on that one, but he's doing something more important right now."

"What's he doing with Ed?"

"David, let him do his thing. Concentrate, this is important; what other bits of information from your captivity can your recall?"

I tried to go about the project as though it was my first telling, but found I was repeating the same details related to the computer, Mystery Man's somewhat familiar eyes and voice, the missing louver slat, and the muffled conversation with Mystery Man and his dad.

It hit me like a bolt of lightning, "Wait a minute; our Mystery Man is Dennis Vincent. He was talking to his father, Barry when I over-heard him."

Jerry asked, "Who is Dennis? Barry? We're starting to need a scorecard."

I explained the Barry Vincent story through the trial and concluded with the death of Larry Spencer and the subsequent investigation and in frustration uttered, "I don't know what they're working on outside, but we need to find the links between Barry, Dennis, Calvo and Alvarez."

Jerry went to the door and spoke with either Ed or Eddie. I expected that the new revelation would warrant the full attention of all hands. However, he returns saying only, "We're going out to lunch in ten minutes. I'm going to wash up." I was underwhelmed!

As a diversion, I flipped on the television to watch what I thought would be the football pre-game show; it was not quite 1:00 PM However, on the east coast it was 4:00 PM and the game was just ending, Jacksonville on top of Buffalo 13 to 10.

Jerry was returning looking fresh and relieved, it was my turn "I just can't get used to these time differences between home and here. Sunday football should start at 1:00 PM not at 10:00 in the morning."

I heard my two other associates return as I was using the facilities and washing up. Entering the room, I thought they had downloaded photographs of Nikki and Nora on the television. They had not. The girls' faces and other scene from a local lake were displayed on the T.V. along with a report that they were found dead, submerged in a murky lake just east of the Red Rocks sitting in the rear seat of a rental vehicle registered to a *Person of Interest*, David Atlas of Boca Raton, Florida.

I thought that we were making progress, but each forward step was trumped by one step back and sinking lower into a hellish nightmare that only Las Vegas could brew up. Feeling like Oliver Hardy yelling at my unknown Stanley Laurel, it was yet "another fine mess you got me into."

Some of the who's were unraveling, but not so much the why's.

CHAPTER 20

SUNDAY AFTERNOON

Life turns on a dime. Speaking selfishly, the gods of revenge just threw me another curve ball necessitating us to quickly develop a new strategy before I was either located by the police or turned myself in. Nikki and Nora's circumstance was much more serious. They were in the wrong place at the wrong time; pawns in a deadly game revolving around me.

We finished an uneventful lunch and were in Jerry's car en route to my hotel. His preference was that we continue on to see Sergeant Cooper as he was trying his best to convince me that it would be better to voluntarily show up and respond to their questions. "There is just too much David Atlas in this story for us to think they won't find you. I'm surprised they haven't called me yet."

"But, if I voluntarily turn myself in for questioning, there's no guarantee that I won't be arrested and, what if there's no bail this time," was my worried response.

He countered with, "Yes, but your chances will be much better than if they have to find you themselves and arrest you."

Still wanting answers, I followed up with "Do you think that I'll get out of there or be remanded?"

"I can only guess, but we'll see Harlan again this evening; another reason to get in there and do it early enough to make his court tonight."

Wanting support, I asked, "Ed, what do you think?"

"I think Jerry is right. This is shitty, but we'll get through it. I'll be there with you all the way."

"O.K., let's do it," was my concluding remark as the three man cortege dropped me off at the Clark County Detention Center, quickly becoming my most frequented stop on this trip.

Still in the parking lot, Ed interrupted our departure from the vehicle by saying that I should be aware of what he and Fast Eddie had uncovered that morning. He apparently thought that it was important for me to hear about it, but I wondered how significant it could be. They were separated from me and Jerry for less than two hours and they were in the courtyard just outside my door the whole time.

Fast Eddie took the lead. "Your law firm has quite the billing software interfaced with your phone system. Ed was able to get me in remotely and the forensic portion, mining the who, what, where and when of phone calls, was a snap."

"So, what did you learn?" My initial goal at this juncture was either leaving soon or being able to see Judge Harlan that evening and I was getting short on time and, understandably patience as well.

He responded, "The three phone calls to Las Vegas entities between 12:30 and 1:15: PM on Thursday were placed by the phone in your office."

"I did not make those calls!"

"I know, Ed has already told me you and he were having lunch out of the office at those times, but the calls were made from your desk."

Resigning to both the good and bad of the situation, I added, "And, Mary said she spoke with *me*. Whoever made the calls had to be a male. What were the two other calls?"

"The first was to National Car Rentals apparently reserving a car for your week-end stay in Vegas and the last was to Paris Hotel canceling your reservation for the week-end."

Hoping for some good news, I asked, "Did you verify that I never picked up the car? At least I'll have that to offer the cops, when I get inside."

Not getting any, he answered, "That's a problem. National claims that you picked up the car at the airport location as reserved."

"That's a lie! Next you'll tell me that was the car they found the girls in."

"They haven't made that information available yet. That's an update of what we know and will dig deeper from here. Ed and I will be working from this end. You and Jerry go knock 'em dead, *Oh excuse me,* do good at the police department."

The meeting was adjourned with us walking inside and them hailing a cab, hopefully not one of the Southwest Desert Taxi fleet. I wanted a longer respite, but it was not to be; before I knew it I was face to face with my pal, Sergeant Alan Cooper. He was more relieved than surprised to see me and I knew at that instant that the boys were right, I would fare better having brought myself in voluntarily.

Although the tone of our question and answer drill was less intimidating, I knew that he was on a mission and all fingers were pointing at me. My reiteration of the abduction was limited as he had heard it before. However, he was not aware that Juan Alvarez was one of my abductors until that interview. Further, this was the first time he heard my claim that Raul, the cabbie, was Tomas Calvo. At our last interview, I told him about the girls and how they were engaged by the conspirators to provide damaging photographs, presumably for extortion. It was at this meeting that I informed him that, Nikki and Nora, murdered yesterday were indeed my unfortunate paramours.

Although Goldstein convinced me that all of this would be better coming from me, by the time I was finished, I was beginning to doubt my own innocence. The mountain of crap that I had to overcome kept getting larger and really stunk. And, he still did not know of the photos, Dennis' identity and other things we had already uncovered.

Notwithstanding the casual ambience, I could not allow myself to think that Cooper was my friend. For sure there were some holes in my story and my explanations and alibis would take time for them to investigate. Looking for some relief, I began wondering not when would this mess best over, but when would I be out free, pending a trial.

Cooper excused himself, saying that he needed a while to go over the information just revealed by our side. Goldstein took the opportunity to ask, "Sergeant, are we free to leave?" I thought, nice try Jerry.

Cooper thought and replied, "Nice try counselor, we have some more questions. Can I get you coffee or something?"

I feared the response, but Jerry asked "Are you charging my client?"

His chilly response was. "I need a few minutes. Chill out."

Cooper served up a great suggestion, I was already so steamed that chilling out seemed like a wonderful idea, but damned near impossible. I had and continued to live in limbo during those three days. Instead of improving, my journey was getting darker and more difficult to navigate. The immediate reality was not conforming to our expectation, I asked, "Jerry, what the hell is going on?"

"He really hasn't given us any new information. My guess is that he's evaluating how he should proceed. I don't think he has enough evidence to charge you, but he doesn't want to turn you loose, not yet."

Under normal conditions, although I had trouble recalling those times, I would have done anything to stall being arrested. However, unless charged soon, I would not make that evening's docket. Accordingly, I would first be arraigned sometime on Monday and not even be considered for bail release until then.

I timidly stated the obvious, "we both recognize that I'll probably be arrested, but I don't want to spend a night in holding."

Jerry was already pondering the possibilities; thinking that if I were arrested later and faced a different judge, we might not get the same favorable treatment. Judge Harlan was only convening evenings and Jerry reached the decision that we needed to force the issue when Cooper returned. Harlan or bust!

This is why even a lawyer needs a lawyer. I was not going to be the fool who had himself as his client. Empathically, he said, "David, this is a mess and perhaps we can't avoid it. Let's just wait to see how it plays out."

"Mess is an understatement!" I was supposed to be on the blackjack tables staging my closing assault on the casino and now I felt as though there was a growing mob outside that clamoring for my hide.

His attempt at offering comfort, "David, I am totally convinced that you are a victim of conspiracy. Now I have to convince them."

Was that comforting?

Moments later, Cooper's donut consuming physique opened the door to our room. Talking as he waddled in, "David, I need some help..."

My ever so quick response, "Apparently, so do I."

"David, you were apparently one of the last to see Nikki and Nora Charles alive. How do you explain that?"

They had the same last name, were they married? I was on a roll! I concluded that such response was inappropriate, so I responded "I didn't know that they were related. Yes, they were the girls my kidnappers hired, but they were very much alive when Juan Alvarez announced that he was going to drop them off out west." I facetiously thought, why didn't I ask what he meant by *drop off*?

"National Car Rental says that you picked up your reserved car at McCarran and that was the car in which the dead *escorts* were found. How do you explain that?"

"I never reserved or honored the reservation," was my short and sweet response.

Jerry chimed in, "do you have a copy of the reservation and transaction details?" Once again, that is why even a lawyer needs a lawyer. I was already walking my last mile and Jerry worked a small opening in the door of resolution. Cooper instructed an associate to copy the rental agreement and customer contract, not yet closed.

I pleaded, "Sergeant, you've got to see that these guys have painted me in a corner and I keep getting squished harder and harder."

My friend, Cooper, went on, "David, I'm on your side, just help me out."

Yeah he was putting on a classic Good Cop routine, but if he was my friend, he would have let me go. I already had enough friends; a good team working on my behalf. "I have answered everything honestly. You have to look into the person or persons who are behind this."

Cooper went on, "Go on, who is the Mystery Man, or should I say men?"

I could have done without the sarcasm, my cup had runneth over with that stuff. I disclosed my belief, "Dennis Vincent and possibly his father Barry Vincent." I went into the detail of Vincent's legal travails and the ensuing death of Larry Spencer. Perhaps he viewed my disclosures as hauling a last minute Hail Mary pass; but I sensed his genuine interest at the mention of the Vincents' names.

"Why would these *gentlemen* do you harm now, so many years after any displeasure they may have felt over your representation of them."

"I never represented either one of them at trial, and I do not know why or why now."

Jerry, intuitively feeling that a nerve was hit with the mention Dennis Vincent's name asked, "Do you know either Dennis or his father?"

"I'm the one asking the questions, but yes I do." His remarks ended abruptly with no further explanation.

Thanks for the elaboration, Coop. I was upset and did not understand why he neglected to tell us more about Dennis. However, Jerry later informed me that Cooper should not have even said what he did, but it provided the hint that we should check public and perhaps so not so public records to learn what he was hinting at.

Maybe he was my friend after all. He could have kept me there stewing all night. He could have arrested me necessitating that I spend the evening avoiding a game of tag with Reggie. Or, Cooper could have received assurances from my counsel that I would remain at the Vagabond or under his personal observation until he needed me further.

Jerry proclaimed that I would be with him at all times and Cooper said, "Make sure he doesn't get lost. I'll want to see him tomorrow."

Jerry responded, "Call me when you want him."

"Let's make it at 9:00 AM unless I call you sooner."

To Cooper, "See you in the morning." And, to me, after Cooper left the room, "That was a surprise, let's get out of here." After leaving the building, he added "it's fortunate that you didn't bring up the Alvarez connection. Otherwise, we would have been there all night."

I had been pinged and ponged over Dennis' game long enough. I wished that he would change balls and give me a break, but I recognized that this would never happen.

CHAPTER 21

SUNDAY EVENING

Nearing 4:30 PM and nearing the Vagabond, Jerry informs me that he had a few things to do and suggested that I should take a shower, put on a change of clothes and await his return. Completely, in character with my alpha male, I asked, "What's on the agenda for tonight?"

"We'll meet with Ed and Eddie at the Fast Man's office and then have some dinner. It's going to be a long night."

"Where are you going?"

"I'll let you know later. I should be less than an hour and stay put at the hotel until I get back. Remember, I'm responsible for your whereabouts."

"No problem, but every time I stay put, somebody dies." How was that for a headline for the *Bizarro World Gazette*?

The solitude, quasi freedom and ability to wash that jail right outta my hair were all welcomed treats. If only time could be turned back to last Thursday. How I missed my safe, predictable and near boring life. It was just over twenty-four hours from the departure of my return flight to Palm Beach and I had no idea of how or if I were going to make it.

My shower was symbolic and spiritual: I was making a clean break from the past and my alone time with God and Dad gave me the strength to move forward. I knew that my story was factual, but looking objectively from afar, I understood how it appeared far-fetched and self-serving to the police. We had to start firming it up with hard supporting evidence.

I went right to the most basic issue: Dennis and Barry. What was the deal? It had been somewhere near twenty years since Barry's conviction and two years since his release. Why now? I found it hard to believe that there even was a connection between my current predicament and his circumstances. After all, I was not his attorney and my testimony although truthful, was both favorable and sometimes not so much so. However, it was not the determining factor that resulted in his negative verdict. Either way it was not me that sent him away, it was not even Larry Spencer who sent him away. He was the one responsible for that one! Was he not?

I was beginning to accept that Dennis' menacing glare; that demonic stare which was tattooed in my memory at his father's sentencing, was directed not only at Larry Spencer, but at me also. Because it has stayed with me over the years, I was now certain that it matched with the nagging glimpses I observed while he supervised my incarceration. Cooper asked it first, but I also wondered: Why was he working me over now, after somewhere near twenty years? And, why not back then when he got Spencer; or not two years ago when his dad earned his freedom?

Did he plan on killing me also? Apparently, he was a guy who did not regard life too highly. I firmly believed that through this multi decade saga he, either directly or indirectly, caused four deaths. Why should one think he would stop there?

I was hoping that Jerry would get back soon. My mind was drifting to a very dark place. I tried to claw my way back to a point in my mental deliberations that it was a choice between two paths. Death on one road and the uncertain future down the other. I did not want to spend any more time on the road to the left and needed to focus on the alternative, resolving the mess.

Concentrating on the road to resolution, I saw interrogations, indictments, a trial in Las Vegas, being erroneously convicted, Elaine filing for a divorce and me spending the rest of my life in Death Valley. Unless, I could reverse that tide, I was not sure I could prevent Dennis from adding another trophy to his case. To paraphrase Woody Allen, "I stand at a crossroad: one path leads to despair and utter hopelessness;

the other leads to total extinction. Let's hope I have the wisdom to make the right choice."

It appeared that either Dennis was going to slowly kill me or created a scenario where my life would be a living hell for some time. I guess that he finally got to both me and Larry Spencer; only in my case, I would have to endure some of the hell and misery that his father experienced. With that, I recalled the spell he cast at Barry's sentencing. "You should all suffer like my dad."

Dennis is a sociopath. He had created sufficient havoc to turn my world upside down for either months or years; who knew for how long. Considering that he apparently killed people at will, he could pull my plug and end it all. Which alternative was preferable? Looking at the similarities, I had a better understanding of Stephen Arky's final days.

Where in the hell was Jerry? I needed company, I needed to be with my rescue squad, and I needed something to eat. I was starving! He must have heard my stomach grumblings, because he arrived and thankfully his appearance brought down the curtain on the current act only to be re-convened after a dining respite with my team in the audience.

His greeting was "I guess you're surprised that he let you out tonight."

"Surprised, my head is still spinning!"

"Even though we need to be there in the morning, I think we're in good shape."

Good shape! Did he go out drinking? I asked "How are we in good shape?"

"If he had more on you, or didn't know about Barry and Dennis, he would have kept us, at least in the interrogation room, all night."

"You must have found out some other information during *your errands*. What's up?"

"I went over to McCarran and cashed in on a favor due me. We'll go over the details when we join the boys." Further, he instructed me to gather my notes, the laptop and the camera and we were off to Fast Eddie's office.

The ride took us back towards the airport and I requested that we take the strip route, "I've been here a lifetime and haven't even seen a casino and besides, the last time I took the Interstate, it didn't work out too well."

We discussed the importance of tying Dennis, Barry, Juan and Tomas together. Naturally, I was aware of the role each played, but that didn't prove they had sinister motives in play. For all the police knew my only connection was stealing Tomas' car and that Juan Alvarez died in a home fire in the vicinity of where I claimed to be held captive during my abduction.

And, then there were the girls. It appeared that I arranged for a party and they wound up dead. How did Dennis or Barry have those reservations at the escort service made? The other calls, to reserve a car and to the Paris Hotel to cancel my week-end stay, were not helpful either. The calls were made when I was in Palm Beach and from my office. My assertion of not being the caller needed an explanation.

It hit me like a lighting bolt! Brent Immerson could have made those calls. He was in the office on Thursday morning and mysteriously had afternoon appointments out of the office. He was gone, but just gone, when Ed and I returned from lunch that day, but why would he do such a dastardly thing?

The images in my office that day were flashing in. I passed his office early that day when he was talking to someone on the phone. Brent offered assurances that someone, whom he did not identify, would be somewhere, that he also did not identify, the next day, Friday. Could that someone have been me in Las Vegas?

Could I really be that somebody? Could Vegas really be that somewhere? He also gave assurances that he would meet his Mystery Man later that afternoon, as they planned. Who in the hell was he talking to? It was funny that I gave his caller the same moniker as I gave Dennis while I was captive, Mystery Man. Of course! Brent was talking to someone named Dennis. I heard it at the time and it registered, but other matters of the day became more pressing and I had not given it a second thought until just then.

My stroll down memory lane in the office that Thursday took the same length of time as our route south on Las Vegas Boulevard. Although I recognized all the scenery, it just blended into a neon backdrop. I was focused on Immerson and why he would do this to me.

I never had the opportunity to meet with him that afternoon and resolve the issue of his marital problems. I guessed it was possible that Jennifer overheard us talking about his double dipping, but I was cognizant of her whereabouts that evening and mentioned this matter to him only when I was sure she was not privy.

If his marriage was crumbling, he had to look to himself for the reason. He was the one who strayed and that was the cause. One should not shoot the messenger, or alleged messenger.

It was 7:15 PM when we arrived at Fast Eddie's office joining him and Ed Sheerson. The boys were working one of those white boards utilizing erasable markers. Their artwork had various names; the usual suspects – Barry, Dennis, Juan a.k.a. John and Tomas in black marker, solid arrowed lines in red, dotted arrowed lines in green and apparently random other matters in brown.

There were Styrofoam coffee cups and crumbled sandwich wrappings strewed on his desk evidencing that this effort had been a marathon rather than a sprint. I wanted to delve deeper into their work as Jerry broke the silence.

He informed them and reconfirmed to me that over the past two hours he was calling a chip owed him by McCarran International's Assistant Director of Security, Eugene Donald. Jerry successfully defended Gene a few years back and he offered up the, *if you ever need a favor* pledge. This was a good opportunity to take him up on it.

Jerry had made his request on the phone and by the time he got to the airport, security video footage of Delta 711's luggage carousel and the taxi queue during the hour thereafter were ready for his review. He made copies of both for later review by the sleuthing foursome, but did do a solo lap around the track viewing both in Gene's office.

He could not find anything useful during the baggage ordeal, but did hit a jackpot on the taxi line. When I entered the queue there were approximately fifty people in front of me. The dispatcher's actions were uniform for all passengers preceding me. He assigned a number slot for the passenger to match up with the corresponding taxi pulling in. In all instances his call signal to the taxi was an upward arm wave motion and the cabs came in filling the slots in numeral order.

As I came up, his arm went down and I was instructed not to the next open slot, but the one at the end of the line. He saw a Southwest

Desert Taxi pull into my slot and the driver dutifully placed my luggage in the trunk and held the door open for me. The driver was Tomas Calvo. Eureka!

Unfortunately there was no Southwest Desert Taxi, Tomas Calvo or Raul Garcia licensed to operate a taxi service in Nevada. Although the trail came to an end there, it was a significant branch on the tree of support for my Vegas saga.

When Jerry finished his report, Seng chimed in, "We found Calvo has a history with false documents. He could have falsified driver credentials in the cab and possibly had a civilian vehicle fixed up as a taxi."

Jerry asked "Do you have a copy of his rap sheet?"

"Yes, and one for Alvarez and Dennis Vincent."

"I think we should order in for dinner rather than taking the time to go out."

Eddie let out "*Déjà vu* all over again."

Eddie pulled out a menu selection from the nearby take out venues and we selected the Red Dragon Chinese for our evening repast. Ed made the selection of dishes, confirmed that such was acceptable to all and phoned in our request.

While waiting for their promised thirty minute delivery, Seng re-walked the investigative steps utilized for the disclosures revealed about Calvo. Using his driver's license and vehicle registration he and Ed developed a personal and financial profile of the man. They were able to check public records for arrests and convictions and learned that Tomas was not quite a choir boy. He had several run-ins with the police, but was never convicted.

He moved to Las Vegas approximately four years ago from Fort Lauderdale, Florida. Calvo had not held a steady job for more than six months floating from one menial position to the next. His was a dance of survival, not one of ladder climbing towards a secure future. His current employment, for the past month, was with an automobile body shop.

A cute Chinese girl walked into the office and I thought here we go again, but then I saw the grease stained bags and realized that our dinner had arrived. Ed, forever the exchequer, paid the tab and tip and we broke from forensics to won tons.

CHAPTER 22

The cuisine was good, but not quite New York good, or even, for that matter, Florida good. The conversation meandered and was somewhat strained as we attempted to keep it light. However, it was difficult to remain casual with the 500 pound gorilla hanging over the room.

The offices of Seng Investigators, Inc. were just off Paradise Road in the periphery of both the airport and the University and housed in a modern office building. My expectation was something out of Micky Spillane's Mike Hammer or Dashiell Hammett's Sam Spade novels. However, instead I was welcomed by a contemporary office with rooms and cubicles for multiple staff equipped with state of the art computers and other machinery I was not familiar with. I was surprised and impressed. As it was Sunday evening, no staff was present, but it was clear that several of the work areas were being utilized and this guy was apparently the real deal backed by many resources and an organization; not a seedy caricature of a gum shoe.

I had never engaged the services of a private investigator; I only had a pre-conceived notion of what one would look like and how he would conduct business. It was a profile of a clumsy, overweight, Inspector Colombo type character. Prior to seeing him in action in his office environs, and judging him by his appearance and actions, he fit the bill. However, I was surprised by his physical plant and impressed by his logical manner of dissecting problems and his ability to ferret out potential alternatives.

Fast Eddie moved to Vegas twenty five years ago from Philadelphia and has been serving the investigative needs of southwest Nevada since.

He built a reputation of being dependable, discrete, almost ethical, and quite effective. He also enjoyed the notoriety of charging very handsomely for his services. His clientele ran the gamut from wealthy socialites to street scum. Upon arriving in Vegas, the Fast Man's credo was, *if you got the money honey, I've got the time.* However, as time went on money was still important, but the requisite heartbeat and checkbook were replaced by the credibility of the story.

The south wall of his office was the home of his photographic trophies. I learned that Eddie had a gallery extending beyond that of a surfer dude. Mostly casual, but many in suits and tie and a few even in a tuxedo, he was photographed with the who's who in celebrity land. The paparazzi extended to political figures of both local and national stature. He even had pictures of himself with both Presidents Clinton and Bush, taken about four years apart. I was on the cusp of having my Bush Trophy, but would have preferred almost any other president. Perhaps even Warren Harding if I had been alive back then. Wow, a photograph of Elaine and me with the President of the United States of America, not bad for a Brooklyn Boy!

All I had to do was get back to Palm Beach unscathed! However, similar to Peter Graves' weekly Mission Impossible tape, I was about to self-destruct.

Ed Sheerson was no fuddy-duddy, but certainly more formally structured than Seng. I guessed that things between them worked out well, they had spent the entire day together and they appeared very comfortable with each other. The ceremonial ending of our meal was signaled as the fortune cookies were passed around. After reading mine aloud, *your best days lie ahead*; Ed came over to offer his support and said, "We'll get through this just fine. Eddie and I made some good progress today."

"I can't wait any more. You guys teased me before the dinner got here, but let's get back to work."

Uncharacteristically, Ed assumed the lead role and called the session to order "O.K. guys, party time is over, let's get back to work."

He yielded the floor to Seng who provided a recap of his and Sheerson's work. His view was that we should focus on Tomas Calvo. He was a low level guy on the fringe of many petty capers since he moved to Nevada from Fort Lauderdale two years ago. The one case that could have resulted in serious problems and time away from Las Vegas was dropped when he cooperated with the police. Either we or the police would have to get him to talk about this one.

There is a definite link between Alvarez and Calvo; they were first cousins. Tomas had been questioned by the local *gendarmes* in two cases involving counterfeiting of personal identification and fraudulent credit cards; the latter of which tangentially involved Dennis. This was truly and fortunately an incestuous mess. That case was never prosecuted due to insufficient evidence and remains an open police matter.

The plot thickened as Seng punched the play button on the remote in his hand and the large computer monitor flashed a video of a man, Tomas Calvo driving a car. Although Ed and Eddie already understood its significance, I did not reach such understanding until I read the recording's header, National Car Rental, and digested the footer: Friday, September 10, 2004, 16:40 hours.

The video was the rental car company's proof that I made the reservation and picked up the vehicle. Although I was scheduled to arrive in Vegas before the car was picked up, my three hour delay precluded my ability to pick up the car at 4:30 in the afternoon. Further, the photograph of David Atlas at the rental security kiosk tendering his license and contact was that of Tomas Calvo.

In reality, the video was my proof that I did not pick up the car and enhanced the credibility of my cab driver story, but how does this prove that I did not steal his car? I had to strengthen the cross relationships of the players and convince the police that Dennis and John wanted it to appear that I had stolen the vehicle in order that I be arrested for the early crimes.

Jerry stated the unstated, "We'll need to show Cooper the photos."

I countered with, "But, what if they were only on the computer and camera. Why ruin it, we have one set and the fire had the other. I would be free of that problem with my wife."

"I know that you'd like to keep them private, but they help our story about Juan Alvarez and your ultimate recognition of Dennis Vincent. Unless they're already out in cyber-space, they won't get out from Cooper and his boys."

I thought about Juan's wondrous mirror image, "I'm not as sure, and don't they also give the police an added theory about the possibility of my starting the fire?"

"Yes, you're right, but all considered, I believe this helps our case."

"I don't think we'll reach agreement on this point, at least not now. Let's defer our decision and move on." How could I be so logical and detached? Thankfully, I was.

Seng once again played the mediator and suggested that we walk down a different road as he addressed me, "Ed tells me you guys had lunch on Thursday, but he doesn't remember the server's name or anyone else who could corroborate your alibi. Can you?"

"No, I don't remember her name; she had red hair, around mid-twenties, but no name. That's all I can recall..................... Wait, the restaurant's receipt may still be in my attaché case." I ran over to my bag and retrieved the American Express chit. Although it was silent as to our server's name, it did contain a date and time stamp which confirmed that the tab was settled by me at 1:02 PM I was in the clear! This detective work was getting easy, or was it?

The blocks were stacking up nicely; we now had proof that I did not either order or pick-up the rental car at McCarran. Further the reservation that I allegedly made with Red Rock Escorts was placed from my office when I was presumably blocks away at Epstein's Deli. The fact that the firm credit card, albeit my individual number was utilized to secure both reservations, suggested that it was an inside job. And, the fickle finger of fate was pointing at my erstwhile buddy, Brent Immerson.

"I knew that we'd find something would be smoldering in South Florida. My associate left this morning to Palm Beach to have a conversation with your partner, Brent in the morning." He was hopeful, that we would have his input by the time that we had our appointment with Sergeant Cooper.

"Why would he talk with your guy?"

"Let's wait to see....... let's drill down on Juan Alvarez."

Seng went on to present a brief biography of Mr. Alvarez. He apparently moved to Vegas from Boca Raton, Florida, approximately the same time as his cousin. His last employment in Florida, covering a span of fifteen years, on and off, was an assistant yard manager at the Boca Boat Basin, a local marina, and he resided at the same luxury rental complex as Dennis Vincent. They were the same age, had similar proclivities with women and often hung out together. They were buddies.

Mr. Alvarez came to Florida and the United States courtesy of Jimmy Carter's Mariel Boatlift arriving on July 4, 1980. Was the date prophetic of independence; his or mine? One would think that the date of his arrival would portend a responsible individual adhering to the principles of America. However, he was much more interested in leaving the dictatorship's threat brought on by Fidel Castro than buying into America's promise.

Like his fictional hero Tony Montana in that South Florida classic, *Scarface* he had no allegiance to America only wanting to further himself. He would go around all day quoting Al Pacino, "I kill a communist for fun, but for a green card, I gonna carve him up real nice." He got his Green Card and commenced his American journey that would some twenty years thereafter intersect with my chart.

His credo was shared by the many that availed themselves of the flotilla to freedom. They were imbued with a hatred for Fidel and a fundamental distrust of America. South Florida offered a familiar tropical environment, with a demographic neighborhood that did not at that time understand, or want to understand their host country's mores, language or other cultural attributes. This established the geo-political paradigm of South Florida for the ensuing decades.

Shit, why coddle Juan Alvarez? After all, he was apparently willing to send me up the river. Although I would ordinarily be the liberal and empathize with his plight, in this case and considering my hopeful Washington appointment, screw him, I needed to think more like a conservative. What an ironic dichotomy. He was a conservative, a dead conservative and the key to this liberal's freedom was to understand him more fully.

The Rescue Squad danced around many issues, but we were once again at that junction of whether or not to disclose the salient facts of my incarceration and the resulting photographic gallery to the authorities. My position was well established. I wanted to shield the photographs of my apparent indiscretion from public view, if at all possible.

Jerry expressed his view, "The photos will obviously hurt Elaine, but she would probably see them anyway and it would be useful for us to establish Juan's role in this conspiracy."

"If I were sure that they were out there already, I would agree with you, but I would prefer to keep them private, if we can."

"David, you've been married forever. Surely Elaine would understand your predicament."

He was Jewish, but would his wife understand? "Perhaps you're right, but let's see if there's another way." I was still fighting; *Ode to the Jewish Husband* recurring theme was that there was no acceptable outcome from cheating. The aforementioned passages emphasize that sex with another woman; cheating, was not to be tolerated. What is the definition of cheating anyway? No doubt, Elaine would see that I had a smile on my face and would consider that *prima facie*.

He fought on, "Juan did have connections to Dennis and Calvo, and we do have to establish that link. They were buddies in South Florida and apparently that friendship extended to Las Vegas."

"Yes, Dennis and John were involved in my abduction. I think we can convince Cooper and still hold back the trump cards. Dennis and Alvarez were practically roommates; isn't that enough?" So went the testimony and cross examination between me and Goldstein until he presented his closing remarks to me.

"David, you're an attorney, but you hired me to represent you. You are too involved in this matter to be objective, we need to do this."

"I'll sleep on it..........are we calling it quits for the night?"

"I'll pick you up at 7:00 AM; we have to be there by 9:00 AM and we'll have time for a quick breakfast on the way."

My close friend, Ralph Waldo Emerson once said "What lies behind us and what lies before us, are timing matters compared to what lies within us." I am a good guy. Why was this happening to me?

CHAPTER 23

MONDAY MORNING

Oh, to think that last week I was eagerly awaiting Friday; my escape. And it was now, Monday, my anticipated return date, and I did not know how or if I would be able to return back to my near-boring existence. This served as a reminder that I had a pretty good life back in Florida which was now about to be stripped from me without permission.

I must have fallen asleep to that picture in my mind. I awoke at 6:00 AM to find that I only had a few hours, extended minutes – about one-hundred eighty of them. This would hopefully be my last meeting with Cooper and my opportunity to turn the gloom to boom and not doom. I needed to get out of this mess. I had a decent hand, but I needed to draw a few cards to make it stronger.

This was certainly going to be an important day in my life. Either I would no longer be required to stay in Vegas and allowed to return to my life in Florida leaving Jerry to oversee my continuing involvement in the weekend's events; or I would be a guest of Clark County, fighting with Reggie, or his brother or worst, brothers, for sexual favors, at Nevada's expense and perhaps pleasure. There was no question as to which side of the coin I was betting on.

Often, the morning's television report foretells or is the catalyst of that day's events. Hopefully, such was the fate of that Monday. That day's reports were largely human interest stories. There were no fires, no deaths, no foreclosures of widows, or other dastardly deeds. I felt like the cat to be rescued from a perch some twenty feet above the beach. My choices were that I could either wait for a professional to climb up and rescue me. Or, I could jump and face the consequences; either a soft landing in the sand or being swept away by the angry surf. Which should I choose?

Jerry, the consummate professional, timed his arrival to allow adequate time for a breakfast muffin and coffee. The time required for eggs, fried onions and accompaniments would have been questionable, and anything more elaborate not possible. He thankfully allotted enough time for two cups of java. The muffin, almost washed through my digestive tract with coffee, was still semi-hard when we arrived downtown: My new home-away-from-home, the Clark County Detention Center.

We arrived at the appointed hour to find Cooper waiting for us at the front desk. Was that good or bad?

His greeting was, "Glad to see you gents."

Jerry's response was, "We appreciate your courtesies. Let's get this thing finalized and David on his way home."

The banter continued, "That would be nice, but…" there was always a but…."I have a few more questions."

And so, my Monday morning commenced. I had tickets for the next red-eye flight, some fourteen hours, but a seemingly lifetime, away. I implored, "Sergeant Cooper, we need to get over this nonsense, I want to go home."

"Calm down David, we're almost there." He always left that other shoe above my head ready to drop. Almost, we were *almost* there. What did he mean? I guessed that I was about to find out.

I knew that I should not trust his ilk, but he was so nice, "What else do you need?"

Such was our dialogue as we traversed the maze from the reception area to Cooper's favorite interrogation room. As though inspired by Rachel, he places a cup of coffee in front of me and says "Give me a summary of your findings since we last spoke."

Jerry accepted the invitation and spent some thirty minutes establishing the nexus among Dennis Vincent, Juan Alvarez and Tomas Calvo. Of course, this could have been accomplished with a five or six bullet point chart, but Jerry is a lawyer, and paid by the word not by brevity. Notwithstanding, he did a fine job.

He did not need a chart. He offered a verbal web of conspiracy among the trio to clearly point towards the Vincents' vendetta to even the score with me. The connectivity among the threesome was undeniable and although the saga of my abduction did occur, we were still expected to prove it. I was in the eye of the storm; a limbo phase providing a certain calm after the winds of turmoil. However, after entering the eye, the storm's return was inevitable and the all clear whistle had not been sounded.

Goldstein was completely factual, stressing the more salient points and adding ballast with others. I hoped that I never had to hear this in court, but it was delivered with the same surgical articulation to be expected in a trial and I believed that it would convince any unbiased individual in favor of my innocence. Yes, intellectually, I knew that Cooper was not unbiased, having a job to do, but he seemed friendly. So did the fabled Colombo!

It was then that the other shoe dropped as he requested, "help me." He presented the scenario that the girls arrived as requested for a meeting with me at Alvarez's residence. In addition, the homeowner and alleged abductor, was shortly thereafter found dead. The girls were also dead. Perhaps too gratuitously, he said, "You should stay here for a while. Whenever you're not here, we have another murder."

Just then Jerry's phone rang and after checking the caller I.D., he asked Cooper for a few minutes pause in order to respond to the call. Cooper agreed and got up to leave the room. Before he could do so, Goldstein demanded that any recording device monitoring the room be turned off and waited until he received confirmation of his request from Cooper. "The room is secure and I do hope that it is a good call. After all, I'm on your side and want to help you."

Looking for any support, I found his last remarks comforting and I got the impression that even Jerry felt the tide shifting.

Circumstantially, I was the common player in the evolving saga; albeit through a conspiratorial staging of events. Perhaps wittingly or unwittingly, Cooper conveyed his key issue: Murder. Naturally, I was aware that murder heightened the stakes. However I was innocent and consistently focused on me, not them. John was a piece of shit, but poor Nikki and Nora. One way or the other, I would always remember them.

As Jerry continued his call in near privacy, I tried to understand Cooper's point of view. There were three murders with three disparate individuals; none all angel and all possible demons. However, I was the lowest common denominator in the equation. Self-servingly, I was not a womanizer and did not want the party that was brought upon me. Apparently, we still needed more bolstering or I would be spending more time with Cooper or his buddies.

Jerry broke into my train of thoughts, or more correctly train of doom with, "that was quite a call." Apparently Fast Eddie just got a call from his associate in Florida. Brent Immerson ultimately confirmed that he made the phone calls for what he thought was a prank.

I was incredulous. "How could he think it was a prank, if Dennis was involved?"

Jerry answered, "I agree. He had better have a good story, but let the local police find that out." We believed that Dennis, the psychopath was pulling his strings, but my defense was better served with police intervention rather than Seng's boy. "We need Cooper to request local assistance in Palm Beach to put some pressure on your partner, Brent."

"Some partner; and to think that I once thought he was like a brother."

Ed walked over to the door indicating that we were ready to resume. What in the hell was the score? Where were we – was I?

Cooper shuffled into the room and wiggled into his chair. I was hopeful that he would offer us some new information about Calvo or otherwise, but he was apparently more interested in the call we just received. He queried, "So tell me, what was that call about?"

Jerry anticipated this opening move and indulged Cooper by suggesting, "Hey Sarge, we do have a nice tidbit, but tell me about Mr. Calvo. He's key to resolving this."

He responded, "We're working on that, he's in the other room." BINGO, they apparently had him and were pushing. Calvo was at the very least peripherally involved in this mess, had already displayed a low tolerance for pain by talking to the authorities about his last caper once it was clear that by not doing so he would be sent up the river. We were fortunate that he was still alive. We had to strike while the iron was hot.

From our point of view, his involvement was not in question. He was party to the abduction, picked up a car with identification in my name, and was related to Juan Alvarez. They had to break him!

Goldstein parried, "What has he offered?"

"We'll get around to him soon enough. Who was so important to warrant a break? Who called you?"

Not wanting to yield his match of wits with Cooper, Jerry indicated a reluctance to discuss the telephone call, even presenting an image of the call's non relevance. He stated, "If it was relevant to this, we'll discuss it later. What other questions do you have?" He was such an actor! However, my life was in the balance, and perhaps he should not have been so cavalier. I would hold his Oscar for later.

Cooper went for and hit the jugular, "Do you have any proof that photographs were taken of your *exploits* with the girls?" I could have done without his sarcasm, *exploits*, indeed. However, in retrospect, I should have thanked him. Although a professional, he was an amateur compared to the inquisition that Elaine would inexorably throw at me and was fraternally preparing me for her campaign of terror.

We were at the cusp. This was the most debated matter over the weekend, should we yield? The pictures both helped and hurt me. He must have sensed that Jerry and I were on opposite sides of the globe over this issue. In order to force the decision, the catalyst that he tossed into the beaker was, "the computer was ruined and we found no camera to support your story of photographs being taken. A picture is worth a thousand words. It would be great to see them, if they exist."

Was he voyeuristic, truly interested in saving my ass, or somewhere in-between? My guess was the latter, but not yet convinced the photos were the trump cards touted by Jerry. If the computer was truly ruined, I might truly have the only copies of photographs evidencing my less than 100 percent but more than zero percent participation. As a result of my behavior, depicted by the photos, Elaine would either leave me, or perhaps even worst, hold such actions over my head *'til death do us part*. The single biggest no-no of the *Ode to the Jewish Husband* – is cheating, even if not intentional.

Although a securities attorney, I had witnessed enough of the proceedings in order to frame the question, "How would the photographs, if they existed, help my story?"

Again, offering more information than required, "The camera would be more important than the photographs."

First looking at Jerry, I continued, "Suppose such camera exists, why is it more important than the photographs?"

"Stop playing games David, do you have the camera?"

I had fought so hard to hold it back, but the dam gates were opened and the disclosures were flowing. Jerry asked for my permission and once granted, sprinted to his car to retrieve the camera. I did receive Cooper's assurances that the materials contained therein would be handled discreetly. Yeah, discreetly, I feared that they would be all over the internet by noon with gift wrapped eight by ten glossies waiting to greet Elaine's return from her cruise.

Yielding, I called his attention to the one shot that displayed Juan in the mirror, proving his culpability; albeit posthumously. The paunchy Sergeant was more focused on the camera, than its output. We later learned that its serial number was in the range of numbers on cameras within Ritz Camera's inventory and one was purchased by Dennis four days ago. Mr. Vincent's photograph and video was taken by another, and yes, more important camera; the one poised over the cash register at the retailer. It was serendipitous that such materials were even seen by the police. The camera shop sustained a break-in robbery after closing on the day of Dennis's purchase. Reviewing the security camera footage, Cooper recognized his mug immediately.

Maybe Cooper was finally showing his true colors, "We only need the pictures to establish that the camera was there. Dennis purchased the camera, it tied him with Alvarez and I'm going to fry his butt. I've been on his ass for a year and a half and now he's all mine." Who knew that Cooper and I had so much in common? Maybe he was my friend after all!

I was almost delirious; freedom was within grasp when Jerry joined the party with, "The phone calls under David's name to Red Rock Escorts, National Car Rentals and the Paris Hotel were made by a Brent Immerson, David's partner. You need to get your pals in Palm Beach to get involved in order to prove that Dennis was the ringmaster of this circus; he's ready to talk. What about Calvo?"

Cooper quickly conceded that "He folded like a cheap suit." How does a cheap suit fold? Poorly! How could that be good? Silly Clichés! He ratted out his late cousin and fully implicated our boy Dennis. It was amazing what power the promise of probation wielded when one faces a lengthy *vacation*, at the state's expense. "You see David, I am on your side, these photos will be sealed and not subject to public review unless the Judge orders otherwise….Do you want a copy of any of the shots?"

I was almost relieved enough to say, "Maybe, one or two," but said "no thanks keep them all private."

That exchange reminded me of my return to the states several years ago from Aruba with a box of Cuba's finest cigars. Although legal in the Antilles, they were not permitted in the United States of America; and were confiscated by Customs personnel in Miami. When I probed about the cigars' fate, the response was that they burn them.

Risking arrest, I said, "Yeah, you burn them….very slowly."

Sensing that we were home, Jerry chimed in, "Can we leave now?"

Looking at me, Cooper responded "Enjoy your afternoon in Vegas and have a safe flight home overnight. Naturally, you'll be expected to be available if we need you further. Keep counsel aware of your travels."

My response was, "This has been a nightmare, but at least the truth was unraveled. If I can go, I'm outta here."

He asked, in true Colombo fashion, "David, one more thing before you leave." Did he have yet another shoe? "You don't recognize me, do you?"

That was what I needed. Just what the doctor ordered, another chance to play *Twenty Questions*. "No, Sergeant Cooper, if I did, it would have been apparent before now. Can I leave now?"

"There can't be too many people named David Atlas and you certainly look familiar. I bet you lived on East Twelfth Street in Flatbush."

That caught me completely off guard. My early days in Brooklyn were the last thing on my mind. "You can't be the Alan Cooper who lived next door, can you? I remember our mutual stamp collections, our experiments with my chemistry set, and of course, the hours of stickball." Of all the possible cosmic coincidences, we shared an ally between our homes and together experienced the freedom of youth, and there he was offering me the ultimate gift of freedom.

We chatted for a while, but soon ran out of things to say. Life does present many long and winding roads. We each took what was important from those carefree days, forming a foundation of our respective personalities and marched forward. "It's a good thing that we had that connection....You're free to go. See you later, David."

I felt like Jimmy Stewart in *It's a Wonderful Life* waiting for a bell to ring evidencing the awarding of Clarence's angel wings. In this case, Jerry's.

CHAPTER 24

MONDAY AFTERNOON/EVENING

It was noon when we left Cooper's Halls of Justice en route to Fast Eddie Seng's office for the mandatory postmortem on the weekend's events. Sheerson and Eddie were awaiting our arrival. Congratulatory hugs and handshakes were excitedly exchanged. I thanked Jerry and Eddie for their diligence, professionalism and friendship. Through my Vegas experience, Ed Sheerson became my brother.

I glanced at my watch and calculated that I had approximately nine hours until I had to be at the airport; certainly ample time for the tables. Amazing, on Sunday I wondered if I was going upstate to get the Chair and there it was Monday and I was seeking a seat at a blackjack table.

Wanting to get over to Paris, but recognizing that I should not be such a cad abandoning my cronies of the week-end, I suggested a parting luncheon, "How about Mon Ami Gabi?"

Intuitively understanding my psyche, Jerry added "We might as well go to Paris...You've been counting the minutes since you got here."

The Maitre D led us to an outdoor table partially shadowed by Nevada's version of the Eiffel Tower. Throngs of tourists were walking the strip. The ubiquitous street urchins were hawking girls...girls... girls; snapping their stacks of calling cards and attempting to peddle them to any accepting walker. A truck towing an advertising trailer passed by displaying scantily clad ladies available twenty-four hours a day within twenty minutes. I had enough!

Ed and I changed seats, removing the foregoing from my field of vision and substituted the potential temptation with an ideal view of the facility's front door and an occasional glimpse into the casino. Having settled the seating arrangements and chosen our selections for lunch, we ordered perhaps our most relaxed meal of the week-end.

The faux French Cuisine was fine; our steaks were properly cooked with a sauce suggesting indulgences of garlic and pepper. We shared several bottles of wine, my first alcohol since the double on Delta, except for that mystery potion served up to me by Raul, a.k.a., Tomas Calvo.

Our fraternal review of the week-end was joyous and cathartic; I had just gone through the worst experience of my life and was on the cusp of getting away from it unscathed. My marriage would be intact, my licensing and practice would be unchanged and relying on human resiliency, I expected to be in Washington D.C. in a few days shaking W's hand.

As the espresso was served, Jerry indicated that he had to get over to his office and the Fast Man feigned that a similar emergency was awaiting him at his. They left the table and gave Ed the opportunity to have a paid receipt from Vegas date stamped at 14:06 hours on Monday, September 13, 2004 for $347.24. I suggested that he keep it as one never knows when such things will be useful. Hopefully, I would never see such an event again.

The entire Paris property conveys a feeling of being in City of Lights and its employees are a perfect complement. The bistros are authentic looking and their pastries are comparable or better than their European competition.. You could ride to the top of their Eiffel Tower and garner an enviable view of the Strip. How could this be in Las Vegas and not Paris? The answer is obvious; a short walk down Las Vegas Boulevard and one could juxtapose himself into Venice with all of its amenities including a gondola ride through Marco Polo's city; or Luxor during ancient Egyptian times, or visit the New York City Slot Exchange or several other venues. The town feels as though inspired by Walt Disney's fantasyland and is enjoyed by travelers worldwide.

The hotel's culinary possibilities ranged from a quaint bistro to a metropolitan Parisian eatery. For those with sophisticated palates, a short ride up to the top of their Eiffel Tower opened into their signature steak house. Bars are sprinkled throughout the facility ensuring that those who were not playing could still be drinking; either is profitable to the house. If one's taste is fast-food, epicurean gourmet or somewhere in between, Vegas provides countless alternatives.

I knew that I had eaten my last bites for this trip. It was time, I wanted the tables. From the top view, the casino in Paris is a circle with spokes from the hub formed by pergolas adorned with vines, pretty flowers and, of course, cameras monitoring everything. The décor was designed to convey an outdoor French countryside feeling. The cocktail waitresses, falling out of the top half of their Franco-inspired costumes, made frequent stops at the players' tables ensuring that they were well oiled.

It was just after two in the afternoon, almost seven hours until I needed to be at McCarran for the Red Eye to reality. I was free of the events and unsavory personalities of the last seventy-two hours, and joyfully, Sheerson was desirous of learning the nuances of Blackjack. We finally reached the original objective of the week-end. I strolled over to the credit window to activate my line of credit and made a bee line to the nearest fifty dollar table. I usually played at the green, twenty-five dollar minimum, but feeling omnipotent; that the upcoming session was destined to be special, I decided to raise the stakes. Perhaps, I should have sought a one hundred dollar game.

We sat at a table controlled by dealer, Lee, an attractive Vietnamese woman. If Doc were with me, that never would have happened. For starters, it was a fifty dollar table, above his pay grade. Additionally, he thinks Asian dealers are unlucky. I have told him repeatedly that his philosophy was bankrupt. Some are good and some are not, and on the following day, the good ones are bad and vice versa for our previous foes. Ed was a rookie and willing to follow my lead. Perhaps he would be better off if he was more like Doc. We would see.

I requested a two thousand dollar marker and Sheerson, using cash, bought in for a thousand dollars. I plunked down a hundred as my first wager and Ed put up fifty. Lee dealt both of us kings for our initial card, giving herself a nine. Round two brought me an ace, blackjack and Ed another face card for a healthy twenty. Lee wound up with nineteen leaving both of us winners with hand one. Let the games begin! Oh wait, we were in Paris not Caesars Palace.

True to my intentions, I doubled up on hands two and three, winning both. One never calls it quits that early in the game. I was up nicely and fully expected the trend to continue. As the French-maid clad cocktail waitress delivered my second *Kettle One* on the rocks of the afternoon, I took a quick count of my chips and determined that I was wining over five thousand dollars. Ed also had a sizable stack of black chips; he had to be way ahead.

It was too early to leave for the airport – we had over four hours until our departure, too early to eat – we were still sated from lunch, and no room providing an opportunity to stretch out and nap. So, we did the predicable thing, continued to play stepping up the ante on my unit bet to two hundred dollars.

I continued to get the most unbelievable cards: Multiple blackjacks, many pat hands and when I had lousy cards, the dealer busted allowing my winning ways to continue. After four beverages, I had to visit the Men's room. Checking my wrist, I ascertained that we were four and a half hours into the session and estimated that the plus factor was in excess of fifteen thousand dollars.

I was smiling, Ed was smiling and yes, Lee had a big grin on her face also. We tipped handsomely sharing the wealth. However, I would not have guessed that so much time had elapsed and I made a mental note to check the watch more frequently. The last thing I wanted was to miss the plane and have to stay in Vegas yet another day.

Upon our return to the table I reminded Ed that we had to leave in approximately two hours in order to get to the airport. I told him that I thought that we had more time, but the clock was apparently ignored as our piles grew higher and the hours flew by. We debated leaving then, cashing in our chips and having a light bite at McCarran. However logical, it was way too practical a solution; we continued playing. However, I was fully cognizant of the time and would not miss our flight.

Lee saved our seats while she shuffled and we freshened up and as we sat down, the final session of this trip began with my unit bet increased to three hundred dollars. Ed increased his to one hundred. Not bad for a neophyte. The shoe's initial hand was identical to our opening gambit almost five hours ago; I got a blackjack, Ed a twenty and the dealer nineteen. Another one for the good guys!

The cadence of the play continued substantially unchanged from the earlier session; rarely losing two in a row and often winning as many as five consecutive hands several of which involving splits or double-down opportunities. It was truly an amazing run, but it was nearing 8:30 PM; time to call it quits. I had to cover the marker and we both had to cash in our chips.

I spent the entire day thinking that the gaming gods would turn against me at any moment, but it never happened. Instead they provided my most successful day at the tables, winning thirty five thousand dollars.

After one last tip and many expressions of gratitude conveyed to Lee, we retrieved our belongings from the bell caps, hopped into a cab, not one operated by the Southwest Desert Taxi Company and were off to the airport, thousands richer and full of experiences theretofore unthinkable.

What an irony my *dream vacation* turned out to be; during my first three days, the worst that Vegas could bring upon me was brought. Such was followed by bountiful fruits of war; phenomenal gaming results on my last day.

The cab ride to McCarran was uneventful. Naturally, I was uneasy in a Vegas cab, but was comforted that it was operated by a recognized operator and one not offering liquid indulgences. Although I was thirsty, I decided to wait until we got to the airport. We arrived at the terminal with less than two hours until our return trip to Florida's swaying palms.

The flight was scheduled to be on time and the combination of security protocol and airport logistics to the ultimate concourse and gate ate another thirty minutes. The final minutes were spent feeding a slot machine in a row just adjacent to our waiting area. As the boarding door was being opened, the hostess announced the names of the first class upgrades; and once again, Atlas came up first name, first row. This was certainly a welcomed gesture of good fortune.

CHAPTER 25

AFTERMATH – FRIDAY AFTERNOON

Somewhere in a deep sleep, I think I heard "Hey buddy, get up!" After I moaned and shifted a time or two, almost acknowledging cognition, he continued, "Captain says we're making our final approach for landing."

"Thanks Ed, good morning." I replied finding myself seated, not next to Sheerson but, next to a less familiar, but not unknown person. Beside me was the guy that I met on the flight out to Vegas on Friday. As my senses became fully awaken, I noticed that I was not seated in first class any longer. When in the hell did they move me?

The hits kept coming and the trip kept getting even more bizarre.

His vociferous response was, "Nice, you snore through two movies and can't even remember my name, it's Joe."

Before I could answer, the Captain broke in with his, "I want to apologize for our delay today, but the skies are clear this evening and we have a spectacular view of the Las Vegas Strip on the right side of the plane. Thank you for flying Delta.............."

"Where's Ed, did you change seats with him?"

"Who the hell is Ed? You asked me to wake you before we landed in Vegas and there's the Stratosphere."

Holy shit! I dreamt the whole thing. No Dennis Vincent, no John Alvarez or his cousin, Tomas, no Cooper, no Goldstein or Fast Eddie, no monumental winnings and, fortunately, or unfortunately, no Nikki or Nora. What else was there to say but, "sorry Joe, I must really have been out of it. Thanks for waking me."

No kidding, I really must have been out of it!

"You were right David, this is really cool." Cool? I was still somewhere between a dream and reality, albeit increasingly moving closer to the latter. It appeared that my dream was becoming just that, a dream. We were approaching the runway with a rapidly passing view of Paris, Caesars, New York New York, the MGM, Mandalay Bay, the Luxor, and touchdown.

The intercom broke in "Welcome to Las Vegas, local time is 8:30 PM We hope that you enjoy your weekend. You may use your mobile phones while we taxi, but please remain in your seat until we arrive at the designated gate. Thank you for flying Delta.............."

As though Pavlov gave me the nod, within seconds I was drooling all over my cell phone. Upon syncing with the local network, an alarm sounded alerting me to awaiting voice mail. Voice mail; as John Dean would say each morning as he was shaving and peering into the mirror prior to peering into his boss, Richard Nixon's face, "What horrors await me now?"

Again, the intercom, "Ladies and gentlemen please remain seated. Our intended gate will not be available for a few minutes. Please remain in your seats with your seat belts firmly fastened."

Almost axiomatically, it is, and in this case was, never easy.

I decided to pass the hopefully short delay responding to my pending phone messages. The first message was from my son, Michael wishing me a great time and good luck; next was from Ed Sheerson informing me that he spoke with Brent and all is well; and the last was from Brent, yes Brent. He informed me that Jennifer found out about his affair from his lady friend, Betty. He apologized for thinking that it resulted from my oversight and closed with a friendly, "We'll talk later."

We arrived at gate D-54 and followed the signs steering passengers along the mile long cattle drive to Baggage Claim. Circumstances slowly confirmed and re-confirmed the reality; I was in Las Vegas and had conjured a fantasy – a nightmare. The details of such reverie were precise, the characters were closely knit into the fabric of my life, and the staging was incredibly accurate, and I was still not one hundred percent sure what was happening.

My erstwhile buddy and business partner, Brent, was a focal participant in both pre- and post-party activities. His voice mail was too tempting to avoid. I had to call him to determine if I could decisively move to either side of the reality scale. It was only 8:45 PM, I would be on the monorail for a few minutes and thereafter would certainly face an additional five to ten, before the carousel started moving. I dialed Brent's cell phone, returning his call. Once again, the time zones got me; it was 11:45 PM in Florida. Notwithstanding being after the designated evening cut-off time for incoming calls, Brent accepted that one.

He was home in bed; not in his bedroom, but in the guest room which had become his new bedroom. I did not feel like comparing stories in a *my dog is bigger than yours* competition. His was pretty bad, but mine, if true, would clearly overshadow a mundane soap opera of marital infidelity in Palm Beach. "Hey Brent, I just got to Vegas and wanted to return your call."

Always wanting to one-up me, he responded, "You obviously did not consider the time zones. I was just going to sleep."

"You're right and I'm sorry, we'll talk tomorrow. Give me a call."

"No, I'm glad you called." Brent elaborated that Sheerson had shared his belief that Jennifer learned of his monkey business by overhearing me at a cocktail party. He re-confirmed his message on my cell phone and acknowledged that he no longer believed me culpable and wanted to apologize. Although nothing new had been gleaned yet, I knew that he still wanted to talk.

I was approaching the appropriate carousel and noticed that it had not yet started its circuitous route. I took a detour into that no fly zone between the interior and exterior facility doors offering both a quiet bunker and a non-obscured line of sight to the offloading luggage of my flight. "Brent, I have a few minutes, what's cooking?" How stupid did that sound?

"David, as I said in my message, how she found out. You were not responsible." Blah Blah Blah "We're going to try to make it work." Somewhere in the Blah Blah, I recalled something about a Marriage Counselor named Dennis Murphy who Brent and Jennifer had seen on Thursday, Friday and would continue his therapy next week. Dennis insisted that their son, Mitchell see his associate, a child psychologist on Friday. It was encouraging to see that Brent's disclosures explained away a sinister motive to conspire against me. However, I felt like a balloon on a windy day; completely subject to forces beyond my control. I knew that I was standing on solid ground, but I did not know in which world such site was located.

Offering my support, I replied "Brent, it's a mess, but if you need anything, I'm there; and that goes for Elaine too." The Three Musketeers: Ed, him and me could make quite a force. "I'll be home on Tuesday and we'll talk then. Go back to sleep and it's good to have you back again."

His well wishes and hopefully non-prophetic remark was, "Good luck David, knock them dead."

The luggage was circling and I had no retort, so I hung up as I moseyed over to the perimeter awaiting my bag. As time unfolded, I could have devoted a few more minutes to Brent's dilemma. However, I felt that ample time was expended. My bag had not yet made its appearance and, accordingly, we could have talked for additional minutes. I still had not reached a firmer understanding of the status quo.

Off the phone, my concentrated focus was on the winnowing offering of unclaimed baggage on the merry-go-round of Carousel Seven. Rod Serling must have been floating over the chamber. I glanced over to the adjacent site and noticed a purple floral bag rounding the far turn of Carousel Five. My bag arrived as the purple demon rounded my neighbor's near turn and once again came to view.

And, so it continued. I selected my bag and sought the quickest exit; both for a breath of fresh air and a fresh look at life. The pace of the city; its rushing to and fro tempo were immediately evident. Traffic was flowing, pedestrians were moving and overhead, the ebb and flow of aircraft was palpable. I felt as though I was finally in Las Vegas.

The taxi queue was long, but the supply of cabs met its demand and the line kept moving. When I reached the dispatcher, he pointed left and indicated that I should take the next open slot. It turned out to be numbered twenty.

Enough was enough! I exited the line running towards Delta's Ticketing counter seeking the next eastbound flight to Florida; city not important.

It was weird, but I started crying uncontrollably. I was drifting between two worlds and needed to get to my office in order to seek Dad's counsel. Or, perhaps I was already there. Washington Irving once wrote "…….there's sacredness in tears. They are not the mark of weakness, but power. They are the overwhelming messengers of grief and of unspeakable love."

Events were spinning out of control. Which was the dream? Which were reality? I was walking down a concourse of infinitely repeating mirrors and wondered where the image of reality began. And, who knew when I would find out?

About the Author

Edward Anchel was born in Brooklyn, New York shortly after the end of World War II. As a "Baby Boomer" he experienced the good old days in New York City prior to moving to the suburbs of Long Island with his family during his adolescent days.

He received his Under-graduate and Masters Degree in Taxation from Long Island University and has practiced as a Certified Public Accountant in New York and Florida since 1969.

He and his wife, Ellen raised their three children in South Florida and are now empty-nester grandparents of four grandchildren and enjoy their life as active adults in Boynton Beach, Florida.

LOST IN VEGAS

Lost in Vegas is a fictionalized autobiography. It incorporates core values of the author, his favorite home away from home and the profession that he perhaps should have chosen over the one that represented his forty plus year career.

An attorney finds himself with a free week-end resulting from his wife's short Caribbean cruise with a girlfriend. Despite several reasons that he should stay home, he decides to go on a four day escape to Las Vegas.

The trip to Sin City turns out to be nothing like what he anticipated. He finds himself in a web of events that prove too difficult for him to navigate by himself. He has to enlist the assistance of a one of his law firm partners as well as other professionals to help him through his malaise.

He travels through the under-belly of Vegas experiencing sights, personalities and venues not ordinarily experienced by tourists. Will he ever make it back to his near boring life in Florida?